I0822405

A HAITIAN WEDDING

DIEUVENY JEAN LOUIS

Original cover art by @UncuttArt (www.uncuttart.com)

ISBN: 978-1-951503-94-9 (Paperback)
ISBN: 978-1-951503-95-6 (Ebook)
ISBN: 978-1-951503-96-3 (Hardcover)

Authorsunite.com

For Haiti

CONTENTS

Chapter 1 1
Chapter 2 10
Chapter 3 16
Chapter 4 25
Chapter 5 34
Chapter 6 43
Chapter 7 55
Chapter 8 66
Chapter 9 78
Chapter 10 87
Chapter 11 97
Chapter 12 106
About the Author 111

CHAPTER 1

Patrick took a deep breath and exhaled slowly to calm his nerves. Glancing up at the Miami Wharf building before him, he could just barely hear a few stray notes of music drifting down from the rooftop venue. This event marked the culmination of more long days and nights than he cared to remember. There were so many times when he was sure this day would never come at all, and yet suddenly it was here.

I wish Dad were alive to see this. He'd be proud. Patrick looked beyond the rooftop to the night sky. There was only one star bright enough to be seen despite the city's lights. *Is he up there somewhere, looking down at this?* Patrick had never been a churchgoer as an adult, rarely giving a thought to anything even vaguely religious or even spiritual, but in this moment, he wanted to believe it all. He wanted to know there was an afterlife, that his father was there, and perhaps one day they would see each other again in such a place. Stephanie's voice at his side snapped him out his reverie.

"Nervous?" she gently asked.

Trying to sound more confident than he felt, Patrick replied, "Uh, yeah, a little nervous, I guess." Stephanie raised one eyebrow. Patrick sighed and said, "Okay, fine, a lot nervous."

Stephanie smiled and took his hand in hers. "It's fine to be nervous. This is a big night for you. I'd be concerned if you *weren't* at least a little nervous. Look, this the most important project you've ever done, and you rocked it. You've got this. Now let's get up there and make an entrance."

With a look of relief, Patrick said, "With you by my side, I'll be fine. You look fantastic, by the way."

Stephanie's midnight-blue wrap dress with split short sleeves and sweeping midi skirt was flattering in all the right ways. Her matching silver earrings, necklace, and bracelet were all composed of interlinked silver circles. She had designed the set herself just for this occasion. Stephanie Durant had come to the United States from Haiti nearly three years ago when she was twenty-seven to pursue her passion for jewelry design. "I know," Stephanie said with coy grin, "and you don't look so bad yourself."

They entered the building holding hands and got into the elevator. Patrick hit the button labeled *rooftop* and took advantage of the mirrored walls to check his look. Slim black pants, white pleated tux shirt (band collar, no tie), and tight-fitting green velvet one-button blazer with black satin lapels was about as close as he had ever gotten to wearing a tuxedo. *I* do *look good, don't I.* Patrick Casey had come a long way from when he was a skinny, nerdy computer geek in middle school. He was the only black kid in his school fascinated by computers and programming.

All his friends in those days were into sports of one kind or another. It wasn't until the summer between his freshman and sophomore years of high school that he had a major growth spurt that also imparted to him a surprisingly athletic build given how much time he spent sitting in front of a computer screen. Now that he was thirty-three years old, his metabolism had slowed down enough that he did have to do regular workouts at home or the gym to maintain his naturally athletic physique.

Pausing at the entrance to the rooftop venue, they took in the scene before them. This was an upscale corporate event where everyone looked as incredibly stylish as the venue itself. Light jazz played in the background. Servers carefully threaded their way through the mingling guests with trays of hors d'oeuvres and champagne. Placed strategically in different areas were three giant screens silently playing a promo video for WLTHY, the new real estate software application Patrick had developed to showcase and facilitate the sale of luxury homes.

Scanning the crowd, Patrick saw who he was looking for, took another deep breath, gave Stephanie's hand a squeeze, and led her across the rooftop to a table with two couples. As they approached the round table, Patrick greeted them with an excited "Hey team!" He was also keeping one eye on Stephanie to gauge her reaction to meeting his colleagues Adam and Sean, both of whom were white, in their forties, wealthy, and a little full of themselves. Their wives were clearly what some would call "trophy" wives in their tiny dresses and too much makeup.

The two couples rose to greet the newcomers. Adam opened with, "Our tech genius finally made it."

Sean opted for a warmer greeting. "What's up brother?"

Patrick could feel Stephanie's hand tense slightly in his, especially as she examined the overly made-up women. Flashing his pearly whites he said, "You know me, I like to make an entrance." He could at least act confident even if he wasn't feeling it for real.

Sean gave him a clap on the back and said, "Well, your timing is perfect. We're announcing the launch in a few minutes."

"Great," Patrick said, turning to the women to greet them. "Ladies, nice to see you both again."

After a slight pause, Patrick went on, "You guys remember Stephanie?"

Looking her up and down, Adam was quick to respond with, "Of course. I could never forget this face."

"Hello," Stephanie said, reaching to shake Adam's hand, but he instead grabbed her hand and kissed it. Although she smiled politely, Patrick could see she was clearly uncomfortable with it.

Still holding her hand, Adam said, "Good to see you again."

Taking her hand back she then extended it to Sean who, much to Patrick's relief, was more respectful with his greeting. "Hey Stephanie," he said, shaking her hand politely. Have you met my wife, Tiffany?"

Before Stephanie could say anything, Tiffany extended her hand, flaunting her huge wedding ring, and said, "So, this is the code puncher my husband spent a fortune on to do some silly website."

After a distinctly awkward pause during which Patrick's nervousness flooded back in full force, he said quietly, "Well, the project included so much more than just code punching."

Tiffany already looked bored as she said, "Oh, really?"

Everyone turned to Patrick for a response, but he was searching for words. "Uh, yes, it's—"

"It's *much* more," Stephanie said, shooting an icy look in Tiffany's direction. "What my boyfriend did was create an entire app from scratch. That means software, which entails programing, procedures, and routines associated with the operation of a computer system, not to mention all the graphics used in the app—the same incredible graphics you see on those huge flat screens."

None too pleased about being put in her place in this manner, Tiffany sat back down in a huff with a pouty expression, which was greatly exaggerated by her plumped-up lips.

Glancing at his watch, Sean quickly said, "Okay, looks like it's go time." Adam downed the rest of his drink and handed the empty glass to his wife. He and Sean made their way up to the stage.

Patrick and Stephanie took their seats at the table but turned them to face the stage and away from the two women. Patrick leaned in close to whisper in Stephanie's ear, "What would I do without you?"

With mock seriousness she replied, "That is an excellent question." The she smiled warmly and said, "You know I've always got your back."

On the stage, Sean gestured to the DJ to cut the music. Microphone in hand, Sean addressed the crowd. "Good evening, everyone. We want to thank you all for coming out tonight. We are so happy to have you all on our team working with us. Our sales agents have had the most incredible year so far with over $600 million in sales!"

Applause and cheers enthusiastically erupted from the guests. Adam leaned over, grabbed the mic, and said, "And don't forget being listed in *Real Trends* as the top-grossing team in the country!" More cheers and applause ensued.

Adam gave the mic back to Sean who went on, "Yes, like Adam said, *Real Trends* did happen, and I couldn't be prouder of every person here. One of the things that helps us stay ahead of the game and always a step ahead of our competitors is our tech department," then looking to Patrick he added, "actually, Patrick, come on up here."

With his heart thumping so hard he thought for sure everyone could hear it, Patrick made his way through the crowd and joined his colleagues on the stage.

Sean continued, "This man right here, this tech God we have had the pleasure of working with for the last two years, has once again elevated our game, putting our company ahead of all the other firms with his latest project. Tonight, we are unveiling the launch of our new software, WLTHY! This app will not only change how we show our properties, but also give our clients easy access to whatever they need, and all from the palm of their hand. You know, when I was twenty-two years old, I was parking cars out front of this place. Seeing millionaire after millionaire come through these doors, I made a decision to live my life on my own terms, unapologetically, for better or for worse. And it was the single best choice of my life. But you know what, I'm talking too much and drinking too much, so let me shut the hell up and let this video say it all."

As the video played, the crowed was awed by what they saw. Stephanie knew how much time and effort Patrick had put into this app, and it clearly paid off. She was amazed at what he had accomplished.

* * * * *

After the event ended, Patrick and Stephanie stood outside waiting for their car. Many of the other guests filing out offered their congratulations to Patrick on a job well done. Stephanie put her arm around his waist and gave him a good squeeze.

Being both amped up and somewhat relieved the whole thing was over, Patrick sighed and said, "What a great night!"

Stephanie murmured, "It was very eye opening."

Patrick looked at her lovingly but could see she wasn't fully present. "Are you okay?"

Pausing a moment before replying, Stephanie said, "Yeah, I'm fine. It's just, watching you tonight made me realize how I've been so wrapped up in your world for such a long time I'm kind of losing focus on my own career."

Surprised by this sudden reveal, Patrick said, "Babe, you can't look at it like that. My success is yours as well, right?"

Stephanie looked into his eyes and replied, "But it's not the same. The whole reason I left my country was to create my own life, not to be in the shadow of someone else's."

The valet pulled up in front of them with Patrick's car. Trying to deflect the direction this conversation was going, he said, "Don't be silly. You're not in my shadow. It's more like I'm gladly standing in *your* light." He kissed her on the check and opened the passenger door for her. "Come on, the night is still young."

CHAPTER 2

The drive back to Patrick's penthouse apartment in West Brickell was largely silent. While he was preoccupied with navigating traffic, Stephanie studied this man she had been dating for the last nine months. It was easy to be with him right from the start. *He's warm, genuine, hard-working, handsome, and mostly humble, except when he's trying to keep up with the lifestyle of his colleagues.* But she couldn't shake the feeling she had somehow allowed herself to become lost in his world rather than establishing her own. *I need to sort this out with him.*

Kicking off their shoes after entering his well-appointed apartment, Stephanie didn't want to put off the conversation she needed to have with him any longer. "Patrick," she said resolutely.

Patrick was already in the kitchen getting a glass of water. "Yeah, babe?"

Standing opposite him across the kitchen island, she said, "So, like was saying earlier, I have always lived on someone else's terms and..." Stephanie hesitated for a moment, trying to find the right way to say what she needed him to hear.

"Babe, what's up?" Patrick asked, as if she shouldn't have a care in the world.

Stephanie went on, "I see how much joy tonight brought you and I want that too."

"So, what are you saying?" Patrick asked. She could see he was beginning to seriously consider where this conversation might be headed.

Holding his gaze, Stephanie said, "I want to live life on my own terms."

Patrick now looked nervous. "Stephanie, are you breaking up with me?"

"No, not at all. It's just, what am I doing here? I left Haiti and my overbearing parents to find myself, and I don't feel like I've figured that out at all."

Breathing a sigh of relief, Patrick said, "Steph, in a minute you won't have to worry at all, baby. This is the vision I always had for us." He stepped around to her side of the island and kissed her on the forehead.

Taking a step back from him she said, "And that might be a problem in itself, Patrick." She turned away from him and headed for the bedroom, frustrated by his inability to grasp how serious she was about this.

She heard him call out to her, “I wasn’t saying it like that. Babe, come back.” Stephanie ignored him and went into the bedroom to change out of her party dress, but something caught her eye. There was something lying in the middle of the king-size bed. As she approached for a closer look, she put a hand over her mouth when she realized what it was—an open ring box with a large diamond engagement ring shining brightly despite the room’s soft lighting.

A thousand thoughts ran through her mind in the seconds that passed between her realization of what was on the bed and then feeling Patrick’s strong arms encircling her waist from behind in a gentle embrace. Was this what she wanted? Could a life with Patrick be different from what she was worried it would mean for her? When would she have a chance to stretch her own wings and fly? She loved Patrick dearly, there was no doubt about that, but there were things she wanted to do and accomplish for herself as well. Would there be room for that?

“Oh my God, Patrick.”

Releasing her from his embrace, Patrick retrieved the ring from the bed and got down on one knee. “Stephanie, I know it’s only been a short amount of time that we’ve been together, but you are the woman I’ve dreamed about my entire life.”

Despite everything she'd been thinking about since the rooftop event, Stephanie could feel tears beginning to fill her eyes. She tried to wipe them away, but they kept coming.

Patrick continued, "I design and create things for a living, and if I had to design the perfect person for me, it would hands-down be you. You have a heart of gold. You're nurturing, sweet, and caring. You are the most beautiful person I have ever met, inside and out. Will you do me the honor of being my wife?"

This was it. She had to say something. She had to answer this simple yet complicated question he had just posed to her. With her tears still flowing freely, Stephanie stammered, "Y-y-yes."

Patrick took her left hand in his, and with his right hand slipped the ring onto her finger. He rose and embraced her, kissing her passionately. Her tears had finally stopped. Sweeping her off her feet into his arms, he then laid her ever so gently on the bed.

* * * * *

The next morning, Stephanie was sitting up in bed, deep in thought. She said yes to Patrick's proposal last night, for better or worse. Their passionate love-making was all-consuming, after which they both fell into a deep sleep. *Was it all a dream?* No, it most definitely was not a dream. She'd said yes, and now it would be up to her to figure out how to carve out her path forward in life with this beautiful man beside her who was just beginning stir.

She watched him as his eyes opened and he smiled contentedly. Returning her gaze with his own, he reached out and gently caressed her face and said, "Good morning."

Stephanie took his hand in hers and pressed her lips to it. "Morning. How did you sleep?"

Patrick sighed and put his hands behind his head, still smiling broadly. "I slept wonderful. I don't think this smile has left my face. Last night was one of the best nights of my life."

Snuggling into him and laying her head on his chest, Stephanie allowed this moment to linger before saying, "Do you think we're doing the right thing, though? Are we being too hasty?" She could sense a slightly defensive stiffening in his body as he took her words in.

"Of course not. My mother and father got married all of three months after they met and were inseparable since then up until he died and—"

Stephanie shot upright in bed with a gasp and said, "Oh my God."

"What?" Patrick asked in alarm.

Her words gushed out in a flood of nervousness. "I-I've got to call my mother and tell her and Grann about the engagement! They'll *kill* me if they find out any other way." Stephanie jumped out of bed, grabbed her phone, and started dialing madly. She saw Patrick was now getting out of bed himself, a perplexed look on his face.

"I'll go make us some coffee," he said as he threw on a robe and headed for the kitchen.

CHAPTER 3

As the coffee percolated, Patrick felt quite pleased with himself. *I'm engaged!* He had met Stephanie not long after his father died, and they bonded immediately. She tirelessly supported him throughout his grief, keeping him going on the WLTHY project even when he just wanted to give it all up and crawl under a rock in his misery. He didn't know all that much about her really, except that she was beautiful, kind, and came to the US from Haiti. She never spoke much at all about her life in Haiti, so Patrick just assumed her life there must have been difficult. He made a point of not pressing for details as it was clearly a topic she wanted to avoid.

Whenever Haiti came up in the news, the stories always revolved around natural disasters, extreme poverty, rampant gang violence, or political turmoil, such as the recent assassination of the president. In these moments Patrick wanted to speak of Haiti with

Stephanie, but the grim, tight-lipped expression on her face watching media coverage her home country made him think better of it. She'd talk about it when she was ready.

Stephanie walked into the living room with her phone glued to her ear. Holding the phone away from her ear she said to Patrick, "My mother and Grann are screaming right now. They said congratulations.

Patrick smiled and called out, "Thank you!"

Putting the phone back to her ear, Stephanie said, "Thanks, Mom." Then her expression changed to one of exasperation. "Yes, he knows… Mom, I said yes. We'll be there… Okay, I love you too. Bye."

Patrick wasn't sure what to make of that phone call. "That sounded intense."

"You have no idea," Stephanie said. "Wow. I had to get off the phone because they had a million questions. My mom's been praying for me to get married pretty much since I was born. And of course, they want to see the ring."

"Well, snap a picture and send it to them," Patrick suggested. "They're going to pass out when they see it. They've probably never seen anything like it before." It pleased him to no end that he could afford to give her such a high-end engagement ring.

Shaking her head in disagreement, Stephanie said, "Oh, I don't know about that. My mom has tons of jewelry."

Patrick responded with a polite smile. *There's no way her mom has ever seen a diamond like that.*

Stephanie must have thought better of it, though, because then she did model her left hand with the ring on it and snapped a photo with her phone in the other hand. She then turned the ringer off on her phone and put it down. "I'm turning the ringer off because I know my phone is about to explode." She took a deep breath and continued, "Patrick, I need to speak with you right now."

Sensing something significant was about to be revealed, Patrick put his mug down on the coffee table and said, "Of course. You have my undivided attention."

"My parents are Haitian traditionalists. They expect to meet you as soon as possible and if they approve of you, then a wedding must take place shortly thereafter."

Patrick considered this for a moment before responding. "Okay. But why so soon?"

With a sigh, Stephanie went on, "As far as they know I'm still more or less a virgin, even though I live with you, and I'd like to keep it that way, okay? This is a big deal for my family, and we need to jump through their hoops to avoid a lot of drama."

Although Patrick couldn't help but wonder if Stephanie was exaggerating the situation, he was willing to play along. "No problem at all. Count me in. You hungry?"

Stephanie gave him a smile and a giggled. "When am I *not* hungry?"

In unison they said, "Cuba 1902!" They both laughed and high-fived each other, loving how they were always on the same page when it came to their favorite restaurant.

* * * * *

The sun was shining brightly on the outdoor seating area of Cuba 1902, but it was still early enough in the morning that it wasn't too hot yet. Stephanie picked at the remains of her food, losing interest in what she had ordered. "I should have gotten what you ordered."

Patrick smiled, took another big bite of his food, and teasingly said, "Mmmmmmm. I agree."

"You're so *mean*!" Stephane said with mock indignation.

A woman walking by suddenly stopped at their table. She looked vaguely familiar to Patrick, but he couldn't quite remember why or from where. The woman said, "Stephanie?"

Shielding her eyes from the sun with one hand, Stephanie looked up at the woman to see who it was, then jumped up to give her a big hug. "Kerry! Hey, girl. How are you? You remember Patrick, right?"

Turning to Patrick, Kerry said, “Yes, I do. Hi Patrick.”

Stephanie explained, “Kerry and I used to work together. I think you met her at some party we were at a while back.”

Patrick smiled and said a warm “Hello” to Kerry.

Focusing her attention back on Stephanie, Kerry went on, “How have you been, girl? It’s been forever!”

“I’m great, Kerry, how are you?”

“I’m good” Kerry replied, then held up her shopping bags. “I was just in DNA. They’re having a huge sale right now, but as you can see I’m still rocking my bangles!” Stephanie had designed them especially for her friend, and she clearly loved them. Kerry’s eyes widened when she noticed the ring on Stephanie’s finger. “Whoa! Are you engaged?”

With a modest smile Stephanie replied, “I am. In fact, we just got engaged last night.”

Fawning over the ring, Kerry said, “That is one beautiful rock. She grabs Stephanie’s hand to examine it more closely. To Patrick she said, “You did really good!”

Patrick was beaming with pride. “Nothing but the best for my girl!”

Kerry wasted no time getting to the heart of the matter. “You got your dress yet? My homegirl has the best little boutique.”

Stephanie said, "Oh, trust me when I say my mother in Haiti already has designers working on it."

Patrick wondered to himself what she meant by designers. *Maybe she has family members who can make dresses?*

With a sarcastic grin on her face, Kerry said, "Well, good luck you two. You know what they say about marriage—wave goodbye to the old you and screw you to the new you!"

Patrick could see Stephanie didn't know what to make of that statement. "I'll keep that in mind," she said with a puzzled expression. Kerry gave her a big hug and a kiss and went on her way.

Having finished and paid for their meal, they were walking back home when Patrick's curiosity got the better of him and he asked, "So, your mom has some people in Haiti making your wedding dress? Like something traditional?"

"Yes," Stephanie responded, "She's had a couple of designers on speed dial, so I'm sure she's already put them to work."

Still puzzled, Patrick went on, "But don't you want something more modern and designer than a traditional dress?" Not that he had any idea what a traditional Haitian wedding dress might even look like.

"Don't worry about it. There are some amazing designers from Haiti, like Stella Jean and Azède

Jean-Pierre, just to name a couple. But more importantly, my mom is already talking about who she's inviting to the wedding. I'm letting you know right now that the whole country of Haiti will be at our wedding. I hope you're ready."

Now Patrick was thoroughly confused. "They're all coming to Miami?"

Stephanie hesitated a moment before continuing, "Well, no. You know we've got to go to Haiti for this, right?

"For the wedding?" Patrick asked.

In a firm yet gentle voice, Stephanie replied, "Yes. We have to get married in Haiti, babe. I mean, I can't get married without my family."

Patrick didn't want to make a big thing out of this, but he did want to know what was behind it. "Of course, but why can't your family come here?"

With a laugh, she replied. "Do you know how big my family is?"

"You've mentioned it," Patrick said, carefully choosing his words, "but are you inviting everyone to our wedding?"

"Listen," Stephanie said in a more serious tone, "my Grann is not very healthy right now and can't travel."

Patrick sighed and shrugged his shoulders. "I completely understand, but I do want to invite my colleagues and some of my family too."

"Yes, but your family is very small compared to mine," Stephanie explained. "It'll be easier for them to travel. And you never even talk to your family, so…"

He was a little irked by this last bit. "Hey, just because I don't talk all day to my family like you do, doesn't mean I don't want them at my wedding. Why can't we just have your parents, your Grann, your brother, and a few friends? We can send everyone else pictures." Patrick paused for a moment to register Stephanie's frown at this idea. "I mean, I don't want to be rude, but I'm also not comfortable asking friends and family to travel to a dangerous third world country either."

The look Stephanie shot him was a mix of shock and disbelief, with a little anger mixed in for good measure. "Are you *serious*?"

Patrick held his ground. "I am."

Raising her voice, she said, "You don't even *know* Haiti!"

He came back with "I know it's one of the most dangerous countries in the world."

"My country is one of the most beautiful places on the planet!" she shot back. "You honestly can't even speak on it because you have never been there. If you would come, you would never feel the same or think the same about Haiti. If you want to marry me, then you have to know and understand them both. My family is a part of me, so you need to know everyone.

Time to de-escalate this. Patrick smiled at her to lighten the moon and grabbed her hand. “Okay, okay. You’re right. And I completely understand. Why don’t we do this: Let’s fly to Haiti, celebrate with your family, and have the wedding of your dreams there, then we come back here and have a small ceremony with my family and friends. What do you think?” He rubbed his fingers over her hand and flashed his gorgeous pearly whites to persuade her.

After thinking about it for a moment, Stephanie said, “I like it. Thank you.”

Breathing an internal sigh of relief, Patrick simply said, “Anything for my queen,” but he wasn’t all certain about this tenuous agreement.

CHAPTER 4

Stephanie grinned like a child on Christmas day. She took the window seat during their first-class flight to Haiti and was now staring down at her island home as the plane prepared to make its landing at Aéroport international de Cap-Haïtien. Holding Patrick's hand since the island first came into view, she now gave it a squeeze and kissed his cheek. Her expression became a little more serious as she said, "So, first things first, you need to talk to my father."

Patrick was all smiles and said, "Of course. I am looking forward to it."

He still doesn't get it. Stephanie sighed and said, "No. In my family, it's customary to ask permission for my hand in marriage, and since you didn't do that, my father might have some words for you."

Letting that sink in for a moment, Patrick then said, "Do I need to be worried?"

Stephanie giggled at his nervousness and said, "His bark is loud, but his bite isn't bad. Plus, he'll be impressed by you, so you'll be fine.

Patrick leaned over her to get a better look out the window. As he took in the sight of the island in all its beauty, his eyes widen in surprise. Stephanie could see he was taken off-guard by the gorgeous view. She couldn't help but smile to herself, quite pleased with his reaction.

After exiting the plane, Stephanie grabbed Patrick's hand and led the way since she knew where to go. As they passed through the gate area, they were greeted with the sounds of traditional Haitian music. Once again, Stephanie can see Patrick is clearly impressed.

"I've never heard music quite like this before," Patrick said with an air of wonder. "What is it?" The band consisted of two acoustic guitars, an accordion, and several different percussionists, one of which played maracas and the others various types of drums. There was another musician who played something that looked like a giant thumb piano, which provided lower bass notes.

Stephanie was more than happy to explain, "It's called twoubadou, combining Haiti's traditional méringue with Cuban guajiro traditions. In Haiti we consider it our national music, but it's mostly unknown in the rest of the world."

When they arrived at baggage claim, Patrick spied their luggage on the carousel and loaded their three huge suitcases on a cart while Stephanie was texting on her phone. "Okay, I think that's everything."

Putting her phone in her purse, Stephanie said, "Thanks, babe. I just texted my mom to let her know we've arrived."

Exiting baggage claim into the airport's main waiting area, a throng of people were waiting, looking for their travelers, along with several drivers holding signs with the names of their intended passengers. Stephanie scanned the crowd but didn't see anyone she recognized.

"Want me to just grab a taxi?" Patrick offered.

Stephanie shook her head and said, "No. My father usually sends Cedric to pick me up."

"Who's Cedric?" Patrick wondered aloud.

"Oh, he's our driver," Stephanie replied nonchalantly.

"Driver?" Patrick asked, thoroughly baffled.

Stephanie then saw a large sign with "Mr. and Mrs. Miami" written on it. While the other drivers with signs were all dressed in suits, the one holding the Miami sign stood out because he was dressed in shorts and a tank top, emphasizing his athletic build. It was her brother Michael. He called out in mocking announcer tone, "Mrs. Miami, Mrs. Miami, please report to the waiting area."

Stephanie grinned and shouted back, "Shut up, big head!" With a squeal she threw herself at her brother for a big hug. Patrick looked on, helpless and confused.

Taking a step back from Stephanie, Michael looked her up and down and said, "What's up baby girl! Look at you, the sophisticated city girl."

"Whatever!" Stephanie said, striking a glamour pose. "Island girl all day long, and you know it!" Stephanie finally remembered Patrick, who was just standing there, looking awkward at this display of intimacy without even knowing who Michael was. "Oh, I'm sorry. Michael, this Patrick. Patrick, this is my brother Michael."

Patrick extended his hand to shake, but Michael waved it off and went in for a big hug, saying, "What's up, man!"

Stephanie could see Patrick was still feeling a little awkward as he said, "Hey, nice to meet you."

Michael was all smiles. "Welcome to the family, bro." Patrick visibly relaxed and allowed himself to enjoy the warm welcome. As he led them out of the airport, Michael continued, "My sister tells me this is your first time in Haiti?"

Patrick replied, "Yes. First time."

Michael clapped Patrick on the back as he said, "Woo-weeee! You are about to see heaven my friend. Are you ready?"

Out on the curb was a black Toyota Land Cruiser with a police officer standing near it. Patrick warned Michael, "Hey man, I think they're about to give you a ticket."

Michael made a scoffing noise and walked over to the officer. "Thanks for keeping an eye on my ride, Marlon. And tell your mother hello for me." He then slipped the officer some money to load the luggage into the vehicle.

Keeping one on Patrick, Stephanie could see he was in awe of this. He'd probably never seen a police officer helping load luggage into a car at an airport. They all get in the Land Cruiser, Michael behind the wheel, Stephanie in the front passenger seat, and Patrick in the back seat behind Stephanie. Still impressed by the officer handling their luggage, Patrick asked, "I've never seen a cop help with luggage at the airport. Is he like one of your cousins or something?"

Glancing back at him through the rearview mirror, Michael said, "Everyone in this country is my family, brother."

Stephanie giggled and explained to Patrick, "My brother knows everyone here. And they all love him. I keep telling him to run for president."

Michael smiled and laughed at that but said, "Please. I am a man of the people, not a politician. But for the next two weeks, I am officially your tour guide." He cranked up the music, letting Lakay by Tabou Combo blare out of the speakers.

I'm in heaven. Stephanie rolled down her window and leaned her head out to catch the island breeze and breathe it in. She felt immediately rejuvenated being back on her island home. When Michael pulled the vehicle into an area with a helicopter pad, Stephanie was immediately suspicious. "Michael, what are you doing?"

"I'm giving your fiancé the best tour of our country!" he said with a grin.

"Mom is going to kill you," Stephanie said. "You know she's waiting for us to get there!"

Michael waved her off, saying "She'll be fine. She and Grann are busy in the kitchen. We'll be home by dinner. Promise." As Michael parked the car and they all got out, the pilot already had the helicopter's blades whirling. They carefully boarded the chopper and put on headsets so they could speak to each other and the pilot. "My man! You already know where we gotta go. Let's hit it," Michael said to the pilot, and off they went.

After flying a while, Michael nudged Patrick and said, "That down there, my friend, is The Citadelle Laferrière, though everyone just calls it The Citadel. It's a nineteenth century fortress with a ton of history. After Haiti gained its independence from France in 1804, one of the key revolutionary leaders, Henri

Christophe, commissioned the creation of the fortress. Tens of thousands of former slaves participated in building it over fifteen years. It sits atop Bonnet à l'Evêque mountaintop because it was a strategic location from which to defend themselves against possible French attacks."

It was like a giant castle set high upon a summit. Stephanie kept her gaze fixed on Patrick to see what his reaction would be to this sightseeing tour. After taking in the impressive view of The Citadel, he glanced at Stephanie and mouthed, "Wow!"

The next sight on their tour was the ruins of the Palace of Sans-Souci. Michael explained: "This area was once a plantation where Henri Christophe worked the fields for the French. After the revolution, he became Henri I, King of Haiti, and had this palace built over the course of several years, completed in 1813. Its splendor was noted by many visitors to Haiti at that time. Much of it was wrecked by a devastating earthquake in 1842 and it was never rebuilt."

Stephanie watched Patrick, who had a faraway look in his eyes. He must have been imagining what this palatial estate was like in its glory days. The pilot then flew them over the southwestern peninsula of the island and out over the water of the Baie de Cayes where the approached an island.

"This is Île-à-Vache, one of Haiti's satellite islands," Michael said. "It was under Spanish control from 1492 until 1697 when France and Spain settled on the dividing the main island between them, with the eastern part becoming the Dominican Republic while the western part, including Île-à-Vache, was ceded to the French and named Saint-Domingue. It wasn't until after the revolution that it was called Haiti. This little island is one of the top destinations of Haiti because it has some of the best island scenery in all the Caribbean, but I say it's the most beautiful island in the world. The waters there are crystal clear. Trust me when I say you've never seen anything like it!"

The helicopter circled around Île-à-Vache and then made its way up to the northern coastline where Michael announced, "And this is Labadee Beach. It's a very popular tourist destination for cruise ships, but it doesn't take away from the fact that it's the most gorgeous beach in the world, and nothing like those beaches in Miami!"

Patrick was dumbfounded. "That water looks incredible. I've never seen anything like it!"

Michael grinned and said, "You will experience that water while you're here brother. I got you.

"Wow," Patrick went on, "They just don't show images of Haiti like this in the media back home. All I've ever seen is extreme poverty and natural disasters."

With a roll of his eyes, Michael said, "If you're going off the images the world shows, then you've never really seen Haiti, so get ready, my friend. Anything you've ever seen about Haiti, disregard it and take it out your mind. I'm going to show you the real Haiti."

"Please do!" Patrick responded eagerly.

Stephanie smiled to herself. She had to hand it to her brother, he really knew how to show off the best of Haiti and did it in style. It made her feel even more pride in her home island. The pilot banked the helicopter and headed back toward the landing pad where they had started. Patrick squeezed Stephanie's hand as he continued drinking in all the sights below him.

CHAPTER 5

After disembarking from the helicopter and getting back into Michael's Land Cruiser, the trio drove through the streets of Cap-Haïtien, a city of around 200,000 people, situated on the northern coast of Haiti. Patrick stared out the window, examining every inch of the scenery passing by him. They entered a neighborhood where the homes were large and luxurious. Patrick's eyes widened at what he was seeing. Michael looks at him in the rearview mirror with a smile. Patrick's eyes nearly popped out of his head when Michael pulled the Land Cruiser into a driveway with elegant wrought iron gates. Michael pulled up close to the gate, rolled down his window, and pressed a button on a security pad. The gates swung open to reveal a massive home with extensive lawns, large trees, and flower gardens everywhere. "Welcome home, sis," Michael announced as he drove to the parking area in front of the house.

A thousand thoughts were running through Patrick's mind. *Stephanie comes from an incredibly wealthy family? Why didn't she ever tell me this?* He leaned forward and whispered to Stephanie, "Your parents live *here*?" She merely nodded her head, leaving him to gape at the magnificence of her home. Getting out of the car, Stephanie took Patrick's hand and led him toward the house. *I had no idea. This is unbelievable. Whatever I was expecting, it certainly wasn't this!*

An elegant woman who seemed far too young to be Stephanie's mother came out the front door and approached them, calling out, "Hello, hello!"

Michael was struggling with one of the giant suitcases. Patrick couldn't help but notice the woman walk right past he and Stephanie and go to Michael, who she embraced tightly. *Must be her favorite.* It did seem odd to him. The woman said, "What took you so long? You were supposed to call me when you left the airport!"

With a sheepish look, Michael replied, "My battery died, so I had to charge my phone in the car."

The woman clearly wasn't buying his flimsy excuse. "Yeah, sure. Seems your battery is always dead."

Finally, the woman turned her attention to Stephanie, a huge grin spreading across her face. "Look at you!"

Stephanie seemed almost shy to Patrick. She looked down, embarrassed, and said, "Hello, mother." Patrick still couldn't believe this woman was Stephanie's mother. She seemed so young.

Mrs. Durant opened her arms wide to embrace her daughter. Patrick noticed it was a very brief hug compared to the one she had given Michael. Mrs. Durant then took her daughter's hand to examine the engagement ring on her finger. Raising her eyebrows and nodding her head as she looked at the ring, Patrick was pleased she seemed to be impressed. She confirmed by turning her attention to Patrick and saying, "You did good, son. Welcome to our home."

Awkwardly, Patrick gave a little bow and said, "Uh, thank you, Mrs. Durant."

She leaned over and gave him a small hug in return. "Very nice to meet you. I've heard nothing but great things."

Still feeling overwhelmed, Patrick said "Likewise. So nice to meet you, Mrs. Durant."

Stepping back to address all three of them, Mrs. Durant said, "Well, I hope you're all hungry because Grann and I have a *feast* ready for you. Please, come on in."

Michael turned to get the rest of the luggage out of the car and Patrick was going to follow him and help, but Mrs. Durant grabbed took his arm and led him into the house. She said, "Don't worry about your suitcases. Annabelle will get them later."

Upon hearing that Michael called to them, "Annabelle is a fifty-year-old woman, mama. I'm not letting her carry these in. I got it."

In the large foyer, the opulence of the house's interior was every bit as impressive to Patrick as the exterior. He felt like he was in shock. It was downright luxurious. Standing off to one side was someone Patrick assumed must be Annabelle, dressed as a housekeeper. She had a warm, friendly demeanor, and was clearly anxiously awaiting Stephanie's arrival.

Stephanie rushed over to Annabelle and gave her big hug. "Anna! How are you?"

Patrick noticed how Annabelle returned Stephanie's embrace and said "Miss Stephanie, so nice to see you again," but did not move from the spot she was in. *Wow. Mrs. Durant must run a tight ship around here.* Anabelle clearly knew her place, which struck Patrick as a throwback to a bygone era. *Apparently not here.*

Stephanie grabbed Patrick's hand, pulling him away from her mother, and led him over to Annabelle. "Anna, this is Patrick my fiancé."

"Nice to meet you, sir," Annabelle said as she extended her hand to Patrick, who shook her hand gently.

Stephanie was now breathing deeply, inhaling through her nostrils, clearly pleased with the aromas wafting from the kitchen. Excitedly, she said, "Did you guys make Paté Kòde?"

Nodding her head, Mrs. Durant said, "Grann did."

Stephanie made a beeline for the kitchen, pulling Patrick along behind her. Mrs. Durant and Anabelle followed them.

When they entered the kitchen, Patrick saw an older woman, probably in her seventies, standing at the stove with her back to them, stirring a pot. She was a petite woman with wide hips and slivery gray hair cropped short.

Stephanie went straight to her, hugged her from behind, and shouted, "Grann!"

Grann whirled around with a startled expression on her face, which quickly changed to one of pure joy at the sight of Stephanie. Her expression turned serious again as she mock scolded her granddaughter, "Child! You're going to make me burn myself!"

They gave each other a long, tight embrace, laughing together. Patrick caught Mrs. Durant out of the corner of her eye, looking at her daughter and her mother hugging with an expression Patrick couldn't quite discern. *Is there a tinge of jealousy in that look?* Patrick was aware of Stephanie's special bond with her grandmother, but now wondered if it was a source of tension between her and her mother.

"I'm sorry, Grann," Stephanie said, clearly enjoying this reunion most of all. "I'm just so happy to see you. I've missed you so much!"

"I've missed you too, girl," Grann said in return with a big smile. Patrick loved seeing Stephanie so happy. But when Grann turned her gaze to Patrick, her smile promptly disappeared.

Patrick felt extremely out of place as Grann looked him up and down, lips pursed tightly together. Then she looked straight into his eyes and said, "So, you're the young man who asked my girl to marry him without even talking to her family first?"

Stephanie tried to defend him. "Grann, he didn't—"

Continuing to hold eye contact with Patrick, Grann raised a hand and interrupted her, "Shush, girl. The man can talk, can't he?"

In a flash the tension in the kitchen was palpable. Patrick realized he was holding his breath and could feel a bead of sweat trickling down the back of his neck. Finally, he said, "Well, ma'am, I wanted it to be a surprise, so I just kept it to myself." Grann just continued to stare at him, so he added, "You're right, though. I should have reached out and I apologize."

Grann let the tense silence continue for several more unbearably long moments before saying, "Well, you must still answer to her father, and you'd better have a better answer than that."

Patrick stood up straighter and said, “Yes ma’am. Understood. It’s, uh, very nice to meet you.”

She narrowed her eyes and said, “Is it? Well, you don’t know me yet, so we’ll see.” Grann turned her attention back to the stove.

Feeling helpless and defeated, Patrick looked at Stephanie. She had a look of true sympathy on her face and mouthed the words “I’m sorry” to him by way of apology for this treatment. He smiled weakly and shrugged his shoulders as if it was no big deal.

Grann turned back around again to face them and addressed Patrick. “Are you hungry, son?”

“Yes ma’am,” Patrick said quickly. “Quite hungry!”

Stephanie chimed in, “Grann, are you making soup joumou?

“Of course!” Grann replied.

Stephanie jumped up and down and clapped her hands. She turned to Patrick and said, “This is the best soup you will ever taste. Grann is known for her joumou.”

Grann refocused her attention once again on Patrick. “This soup is a symbol of freedom. It is tradition to have it every New Year here in Haiti as a tribute to Haitian independence in 1804. Black slaves were not allowed to drink this soup as it was a delicacy meant only for French slave masters. Haiti may not be the richest country, but we’re the first black republic. We may be suffering but we're children of revolutionaries. Joumou soup reflects all of this."

Patrick smiled and said, "Now I really can't wait to try some!"

Grann turned to Stephanie and said, "I'm going to give *you* ten bowls, girl. You are too skinny!"

Rolling her eyes, Stephanie responded, "I'm fine Grann. I just work out every day, that's all."

To Patrick, Grann said, "What are you feeding her up there in Miami, hmm?"

With an indignant look to Grann, Stephanie said, "I eat everything, trust me, just not all the fried foods people eat here."

Patrick added, "Yes, she *loves* to eat, so food is not the issue."

The look Grann shot him shut Patrick up right quick as she said, "She's all bones! You like bones?

"Well, I—" Patrick said, flustered.

Grann went on, "A *real* woman has a curvy body, not a body like a little girl. But it's okay, I will fatten you up while you're here, my dear."

Patrick noticed Mrs. Durant must have reached as much as she could take of her mother-in-law and said, "Patrick, why don't you come with me and let me take you to meet my husband."

Trying to hide his relief, Patrick said "Sure!" with a little too much gusto.

A young woman Patrick thought was probably in her twenties burst into the kitchen screaming in delight. She had cocoa skin and a bubbly Haitian personality. "Oh my God! You are finally here!"

Stephanie was overjoyed to see her dear friend. "Yes, girl, it's so good to see you! Patrick, this is my best friend-slash-sister-slash-bodyguard-slash—"

"Slash *freeloader*," Michael chimed in with an impish grin.

Lauren gave Michael a coy look and said, "You wish, boy!"

"—Lauren," Stephanie went on. "And this is my fiancé, Patrick."

"Nice meeting you," Patrick said to Lauren.

Mrs. Durant cleared her throat and said, "I hate to interrupt, but Mr. Durant is awaiting Patrick's arrival."

Patrick gave Stephanie a peck on the cheek and she whispered "Good luck" to him. The worried look she gave him had Patrick wondering just what he was in for as Mrs. Durant took his arm and led him out of the kitchen.

CHAPTER 6

After Mrs. Durant led Patrick away, Lauren gave Grann a big hug and said, "Hey Grann!"

Grann said, "Hey, baby." Grann locked eyes with Stephanie for a moment, then burst into raucous laughter. "Did you see that poor boy's face?"

Stephanie couldn't help herself and laughed as well. "You are just *terrible*, Grann."

"Well, I had to test him out and see how strong he is," Grann said with mock indignation.

"He's very nice," Stephanie went on, "You're going to love him."

"I don't need to love him," Grann explained, "I just need *you* to be happy."

* * * * *

Patrick followed Mrs. Durant out to a big, beautiful deck overlooking the ocean. Sitting at a table was a distinguished-looking man in his fifties, obviously

Stephanie's father. In one hand is a half-smoked cigar held over an ashtray. In the other hand was the latest issue of the luxury lifestyle magazine, the *Robb Report*. Patrick was familiar with it because he enjoyed reading it himself.

As Mrs. Durant and Patrick step out onto the deck, Mr. Durant deliberately sets down both cigar and magazine and slowly stands to greet Patrick.

Mustering his courage, Patrick stepped forward confidently, extended his hand, and said, "Hello, sir. Very nice to meet you."

Mr. Durant took his time looking Patrick up and down. After a long moment of letting Patrick's hand hover uncomfortably in mid-air, he finally looked Patrick directly in his eyes, grabbed his hand firmly, and said, "So, this is the man who asked my daughter to marry him without talking to me first."

Mortified, Patrick said, "Sir, let me please apologize for that. I understand it was wrong of me to do so and I'm sorry." An awkward silence ensues.

Out of the corner of his eye, Patrick noticed Mrs. Durant took the opportunity to discreetly make an exit. "Well, I'm going to let you two speak while I go help Grann get dinner ready."

Finally, Mr. Durant uttered a single word, "Sit" as he sat back down and took up his cigar again.

Trying to regain his footing, Patrick took a seat at the table, sitting tall and making eye contact with

Mr. Durant. "Again sir, my apologies. In hindsight, it was bad judgement. I didn't know if Stephanie even wanted to marry me, so in my mind I wanted to find that out first before I consulted with her family. I see now it wasn't the best idea. I just want you to know I meant no disrespect to you or your family in any way. I just made a poor decision."

Maintaining a completely stoic demeanor, Mr. Durant said, "Yes, a very bad decision, especially since Miami is so close. I could easily have taken a plane to come there, or I could have sent a plane to bring you here.

Patrick wanted to make this right, if at all possible. *Time to eat crow.* "I'm new at all of this so it's a huge learning lesson, but I am hoping now that I'm here, you can take time to get to know me and that I can have your blessing to marry your daughter."

Mr. Durant considered this statement for several moments before saying, "Good. Because if you ever touch or harm my daughter in any way, I have people who can pay you a visit and make sure you're never seen again." Mr. Durant glared at him without blinking.

Is he for real? Patrick's confident façade was quickly crumbling. He could feel beads of sweat forming on his forehead and his heart was pounding in his chest.

Finally, Mr. Durant began laughing. "You can relax, son, and stop sweating. That was a joke."

Patrick tried to join in the laughter, but all he could manage was a weak chuckle that conveyed his relief rather than any amusement. *Okay, maybe this can be salvaged after all.* Then the interrogation began.

"What do you do for a living, Patrick?" Mr. Durant asked.

"I create software for fortune five hundred companies and manage systems for their businesses to run effectively. Right now, I'm working with a luxury real estate firm that is one of the top agencies in the world."

Mr. Durant seemed distinctly underwhelmed. "So, you're a code puncher?"

Patrick was sick of people reducing his expertise to the tired old "code puncher" label, but this was not a situation where he wanted to get up on a soapbox about his career. Instead, he just said, "Not quite, sir."

Not pausing for further details, Mr. Durant asked, "Did my daughter tell you what I do?"

Patrick opted for total honesty in answering this question. "Honestly, sir, all she ever said was you were a businessman. She never even mentioned you were this successful," he said, gesturing to the property around them.

"Yes, Stephanie doesn't like to talk about her family's success and is very uncomfortable even taking money from us," Mr. Durant explained. After pausing a moment, he added, "I wish her brother was more like her in that regard."

Although Patrick had no idea what Mr. Durant meant regarding Michael, he didn't dwell on it. He was just relieved he and Mr. Durant had finally broken the ice a bit. It still felt like he was attempting to navigate very tricky waters, though.

Mr. Durant continued, "I own multiple companies, but my most lucrative businesses are hotels and cruise ships. My hotels have been voted the top luxury stays in Haiti for the last nine years running."

Once again Patrick was stunned by how much he didn't know about Stephanie's family. "Wow! That's incredible."

"Yes," Mr. Durant stated matter-of-factly, "Tomorrow, you'll spend the day with me so you can see how I operate."

Now we're cooking with gas. Perfect. "I'd love that. Thank you."

Mr. Durant picked up a lighter that was on the table and fiddled with it, flipping it open and closed, as if considering what he wanted to say next. At last he said, "Listen, son, I don't want my daughter to want for anything, okay? I want her to be loved, supported, and financially secure. If you can promise to do all those things, then you have my blessing."

Patrick was relieved to finally be addressing the main objective of this meeting. "Sir, I can assure you I want nothing more than to make her very happy.

Flipping the lighter shut one final time with a definitive *click*, Mr. Durant laid it back on the table and said, "Good. We must have some rum to toast your engagement." He waved his arm and Annabelle quickly stepped out on the deck from inside the house.

Patrick noticed Anabelle came out already holding a tray with glasses and a bottle of rum. Anabelle expertly put the glasses on the table and poured the rum as if she had done this a thousand times. *She must be used to him having meetings out here.*

"Thank you," Mr. Durant said to Annabelle with a slight nod of his head.

"Yes, thank you Annabelle," Patrick quickly added.

Mr. Durant gestured toward his glass and said, "This is Toast 1804 Rum. Have you ever had it?"

"No, sir, I haven't," Patrick replied.

"The company is a family-owned business that started back in the 1800s," Mr. Durant explained. The rum is produced directly from sugar cane juice. And it's one of Haiti's oldest companies."

Examining the rum in his glass, all Patrick could think to say was, "Nice."

Mr. Durant relit his cigar, then raised his glass to Patrick, who followed suit. After their glasses clinked, they each took a sip of the rum. It was much stronger than Patrick was expecting it to be, and he choked on it a little bit, much to Mr. Durant's amusement. "Now that we've gotten all that out of the way, I have an even more important question for you."

Now what? Patrick thought he'd gotten through the toughest part of this challenge. He had no idea what else might be on Mr. Durant's agenda. "Okay."

Back in his deadpan stoic mode, Mr. Durant said, "Since you're a successful tech guy and are now about to be a part of this family, I need you to hack my competitors' accounts for me. Can you do that?"

Patrick froze, once again not knowing whether Mr. Durant was being serious or not. *What should I say here that won't make me look like a complete idiot?*

Luckily, Mr. Durant didn't wait for a response. "Hah! That's another joke. Got you *again*!"

This time Patrick was able to laugh a little more freely along with Mr. Durant, but he wouldn't be sad to have this meeting come to an end sooner than later. It felt like he was trying to pick his way through a minefield.

* * * * *

The large table in the formal dining room was gorgeously set, as if it were a dinner for royalty. Replete with fine porcelain dinnerware, crystal glassware, and gleaming silverware, the table was crowded with a vast array of Haitian dishes. Mr. Durant sat at the head of the table, and Mrs. Durant was at the other end. On one side of the table were Grann and Michael, and on the other side were Patrick, Stephanie, and Lauren. Stephanie's eyes are wide with excitement as she anticipates digging into all the food she's been missing so much.

Annabelle appeared, escorting a young woman into the dining room. She is a dark-skinned beauty with a tomboyish look about her. "Hello everyone! Hey, Steph!"

Stephanie rose and hugged the woman and said, "Hey, Joseline! This is Patrick, my fiancé. Patrick, this is Joseline, Michael's lover-girl."

"Nice to meet you," Patrick said. His mouth was watering looking at all the beautiful food on the table.

Joseline took the open place next to Michael. Mrs. Durant spoke up, saying, "Annabelle, please make sure Patrick has a little bit of everything so he can taste every bit of our cuisine.

Patrick nodded in agreement. "Yes, please! And thank you, Annabelle."

"Child," Grann addressed Stephanie, "you need to cook these dishes back home. They will help you stay supple so you can have children."

Stephanie smiles adoringly at her grandmother and said, "Yes, Grann."

"Patrick, have you ever eaten Haitian food?" Mr. Durant asked. "I'm sure there are plenty of Haitian restaurants in Miami."

Patrick could only nod his head because his mouth was already full of food. After swallowing he said, "Yes, I have. I've had it a couple of times but honestly, nothing like this."

"Sadly, Patrick is all about high-end restaurants," Stephanie said, giving Patrick a coy look. "All the popular American spots." She rubbed his back lovingly to indicate she was just poking fun at him.

Michael chimed in, "Oh no, brother, that's tragic. You have food from Cuba, Venezuela, the Dominican Republic, Puerto Rico, all right there in Miami, and you eat *that*?"

Patrick laughed but defended himself. "Hey now, there's nothing wrong with a good New York strip."

"True," Michael responded, "but come on, man. You've got to taste some worldly cuisines. You're missing out, brother.

Mrs. Durant smiled and said, "Well, maybe Stephanie can start cooking more at home to get his taste buds on the right track.

Stephanie rolled her eyes at that, but Grann threw her hands up in celebration and said, "Wonderful idea!"

Mr. Durant turned to Patrick and asked, "Will we meet any of your business colleagues at the wedding?"

Shaking his head, Patrick replied, "No, unfortunately. They won't be traveling all the way here." Patrick had to be careful here, recalling how he said he wouldn't invite his family or friends or work colleagues to travel to a "dangerous third-world nation" to attend the wedding.

With a surprised expression on his face, Mr. Durant said, "No? Aren't they your friends as well?

Stephanie jumped in for the save and said, "Patrick's colleagues are really busy right now and trying to get everyone to take off work at the same time seemed a little challenging, so we decided to have the big wedding here with my family."

Grateful for her response, Patrick added, "Besides, I wanted to see Haiti and meet her entire family. But when we get back to Miami, we're going to have a small, intimate ceremony with just my, friends and some of my family."

Mr. Durant considered this for a moment and said, "Two weddings? It's not a bad idea. Expensive, but not a bad idea.

"I think it's a lovely idea," Mrs. Durant said. "I'll come to that ceremony, too. I can help plan everything."

Patrick glanced at Stephanie, who smiled politely, but he could sense she was not at all pleased with the idea of her mom being involved in the Miami ceremony.

Mrs. Durant continued, "I do have a couple of friends in Miami. I can help you find a dress there too because you obviously can't wear the same dress twice."

Stephanie nodded her head but was very focused on her food. Patrick didn't understand what the tension was between mother and daughter, but it was clearly something Stephanie couldn't get past easily. She was barely maintaining her composure.

Michael attempted to steer the conversation in a different direction. "So, Patrick, tomorrow after you meet my band, I'm going to take you to eat some of the best street food to be found in Haiti. We'll play some music for you, then I'll take you to some hideouts the average tourist would never see. I know them all and trust me, after you try real Haitian street food, you'll never even think about another American dish."

Patrick laughed at that and said, "Okay, fine."

Mr. Durant, however, said, "Ah, but Patrick is coming with me tomorrow to see the company and all our businesses so he can get a better idea of what I do and how this family runs." When he notices Michael's demeanor become sullen, he added, "Why don't you join us? You haven't been to any of the offices in years. Maybe you should come too so you can see how these family businesses runs as well."

Reading the table, Patrick could see everyone knew this was a dig at Michael, who was wiping his mouth with his napkin as if he were going to get up and leave.

Stephanie tried to save him. "Ooh, that's a great idea. On the way you can point out more landmarks and hot spots to Patrick. I mean, you said you were going to be his personal tour guide, right?"

Michael considered this for a moment. Patrick could see what Stephanie was trying to do, so he tried to help by adding, "Yes! I'd love that." He felt bad for him being put on the spot by his father in such an uncomfortable way.

Mr. Durant nodded his head with a smile and said, "Great. We'll leave here at eight o'clock sharp in the morning."

Patrick watched as Stephanie discreetly caught her brother's attention and made a funny face at him, which got him to finally smile, easing the tension.

CHAPTER 7

A knock on the door of his bedroom startled Patrick awake. It took him a moment to remember where he was—in Haiti at the magnificent Durant residence. The knock sounded again, this time a bit louder than before. He pulled himself up and out of the incredibly comfortable king-size bed, stretching and yawning as he sleepily made his way over to the door and opened it a little to see who was there.

Standing before him was Annabelle with a tray of coffee, croissants, and tropical fruits. "Good morning Mr. Patrick."

Patrick rubbed his and yawned as he said, "Good morning, Annabelle."

They both just stand there for a moment, Patrick not realizing he needed to let her come into the room, so she said, "Mr. Durant will be ready to leave in an hour so you must be ready then as well. May I please set your breakfast down?"

Finally getting a clue, Patrick swung the door open wide for her and said, "Oh. Of course. Thank you." Still trying to get his bearings, Patrick glanced around the room and added, "Do you happen to know where Stephanie is?" It did seem foolish to him they weren't sharing a room here. After all, they lived together in Miami. Still, keeping up appearances seemed to be important in the Durant household, so he was willing to play along.

Annabelle clearly thought it was ridiculous as well. "Yes. Her mother is very excited and couldn't sleep. Therefore, Stephanie can't sleep either," which made Patrick smile knowingly. As Annabelle headed toward the door she added, "If there is anything else you need, Mr. Patrick, please let me know."

"I will. Thanks again, Annabelle." Patrick went to the large windows of the bedroom and opened the curtains to take in the magnificent ocean view before preparing himself for the day ahead.

* * * * *

In one of the home's living rooms, Stephanie sits amidst a chaotic jumble of fabric swatches, wedding dress pictures from magazines, and a pad of paper with what seems to her to be an impossibly long list of names neatly written in her mother's handwriting.

Her mom was excitedly shuffling through the fabrics and wedding gown pictures while Grann looked on from a nearby chair, peacefully knitting. Stephanie frowned as she flipped through page after page of names. "Mother, there are over eight hundred people on this list!"

"And, so what?" her mother responded with a shrug of her shoulders.

"So what?" Stephanie echoed. "I don't even know half these people, that's what!"

"They are family," her mom stated matter-of-factly. "Your cousins, longtime friends, that's all."

Stephanie was already feeling exasperated. "So now I have eight hundred cousins?"

Her mother took on a firmer tone as she said, "Listen. We have already told so many people and if only some get invited and others don't, it'll be bad."

Stephanie was quite sure she heard Grann let out a chuckle at this exchange between her daughter and granddaughter at the same moment her sharp-looking, well-groomed fiancé strolled into the room.

Sensing an opportunity to get a break from her mother, Stephanie jumped up and said, "Good morning!"

"Hey, good morning, beautiful," Patrick replied and gave his fiancée a kiss. Addressing the other women, he added, "Good morning, ladies."

In unison her mom and Grann smiled and said, “Hello.”

Looking around the room, Patrick asked “What are you guys up to in here?”

Stephanie rolled her eyes, exhaled deeply, and said, “Wedding stuff.”

Her mother was more specific. “We were just going over the guest list for the wedding.”

“Yep. Fun stuff,” Stephanie said, then leaned in close to Patrick and whispered, “I should have listened to you and had the Miami wedding.”

Patrick chuckled and kissed her on the forehead, saying, “Nah, it’s good we came here. I’m already loving it.

Stephanie sighed and hugged him one more time for moral support.

Turning again to Grann and Mrs. Durant, Patrick said, “I’m about to take off with Mr. Durant. I guess I’ll see you all at dinner.”

A lightbulb went off in Stephanie’s head. She grabbed Patrick’s hand, squeezed it hard and said, “You know, I could come with you, help show you around.”

Her mom must have heard this last bit because she immediately said, “No, no. There are six cakes being delivered this morning that you need to taste, plus we need to go over the menu.”

Stephanie makes a sad face and mouths the words *six cakes* to Patrick. Once again he laughed, but she could sense he felt sorry for her too. As well he should. This was a nightmare.

Patrick said, "Okay, have a great day, ladies." He gave Stephanie one last kiss and made his exit.

Without missing a beat, her mom was right behind her with a couple fabric swatches and said, "I like this color combination. I think we would all look very nice in this."

I'm so over this already. Stephanie looked to Grann for some support, but she merely winked at her and continued knitting. "Whatever you like, mother," she said in a resigned voice as her mom walked her back over to the couch to sit down and look at more fabrics.

* * * * *

As Patrick walked out the front door of the house, two primary things caught his attention. The first was Mr. Durant looking sharp in a very nice suit, and the second was a silver Toyota Land Cruiser gleaming in morning sun like it had just been driven here from the dealership lot. Patrick looked good in nice pants and a crisp button-down shirt, but he still felt woefully underdressed to spend a day with Mr. Durant learning about his businesses. "Good morning, Mr. Durant."

"Good morning," Mr. Durant said as he straightened his suit. "How did you sleep?"

"I slept like a baby," Patrick replied. "Best sleep I've had in a long time actually."

Mr. Durant was all business. "Good, because we have a long day ahead of us."

When Michael came out to join them, Patrick couldn't believe his eyes. Michael was dressed in a tank top, colorful shorts, and Nike sneakers, drinking juice out of a jar. *Is he trying to get under his dad's skin?*

Mr. Durant's steely expression confirmed it was working. He looked his son up and down and finally said, "Are you going to wear that?"

Michael looked himself over and said, "Yeah, why? What's wrong with this?"

With an exasperated sigh, Mr. Durant simply said, "Come on." He walked around to the driver's side and got in. Michael hopped in the back. Patrick shrugged and took the front passenger seat next to Mr. Durant.

They drive for a while, eventually arriving to a luxury hotel called Château 1804. It stood out from other properties because it was both taller and more modern than other hotels they had driven by. The parking lot had many exotic high-end cars in it. As Mr. Durant pulled the Land Cruiser into the valet area, several young men in red vests who had been chatting with each other scrambled to attention when they realized who just arrived. As Mr. Durant got out of the car, one of the guys approached the driver-side door and said, "Good morning Mr. Durant."

Barely acknowledging the valet's presence, Mr. Durant said, "Morning. Keys are in the car," and went on his way.

After Patrick and Michael get out of the car, Patrick is awestruck as he looks up at the impressive building before him. He grabbed Michael's shoulder and said, "Wow. This is incredible."

Michael rolled his eyes and said, "Whatever." Patrick could see he had zero interest in any of this. In fact, he seemed bored by it all.

* * * * *

The living room where Stephanie, her mother, and Grann had previously been working on wedding plans was now full of women. Stephanie did recognize most of them. These were the prominent mothers and grandmothers of Haiti. On a large table sat six huge, beautifully decorated wedding cakes on cake stands, along with a large selection of sample dishes, each clearly labeled to identify what they were. The room is full of sound as the women mingle and chat up a storm with each other. Finally, Stephanie's mom clapped her hands to get everyone's attention. She was clearly in her element hosting this gathering.

"Ladies! Thank you so much for your time and energy with all these amazing cakes and dishes." Gesturing to Stephanie, she continued, "Stephanie, these women took their time to make this food so you can try all of it and decide what you want served at the wedding."

Stephanie smiled at all the women and said, "Thank you all so much." It was a bit overwhelming, but she was truly grateful for the efforts of so many prominent women.

Her mom went on, "You can start with the cakes. Taste them and pick the top three. The ones you like we'll save for Patrick to taste as well when he returns."

Oh boy, here we go. Stephanie was feeling the pressure now because all eyes were on her.

Her mom was still giving instructions. "After you taste the cakes, then taste each of those other dishes so we know which ones we're going to have as the appetizers."

Stephanie couldn't take it anymore. The level of anxiety she now felt was too much. "Can you guys excuse me please? I need to use the bathroom." She needed to get out of that room before she had a full-on panic attack.

Her mom looked at her with a questioning expression, then gave her head a slight nod of assent as she said, "Yes, go and come right back. I'll have Annabelle begin cutting the cakes in the meantime." Annabelle dutifully began cutting sample slices of one of the cakes, each one expertly laid on a dainty porcelain dessert plate.

Stephanie made a beeline for the nearest bathroom. As with every other room in the house, it is well-appointed and luxurious. She didn't really need to use the bathroom, other than as an escape from the living room and her mother. She pulled her cell phone out of her pocket and dialed her best friend, Lauren. When she answered, Stephanie said, "Girl, where *are* you? I thought you were going to be here hours ago!"

"Relax, baby girl, I'm on my way now," Lauren said. "I'll be there in a bit, okay?"

Relieved, Stephanie smiled and said, "Wonderful. I'll see you soon!" She lingered a bit longer in the bathroom than she needed to, but finally splashed a little water on her face, took a deep breath, and returned to the living room.

She dutifully took tiny bites of each cake, and each dish. Everything she tasted was magnificent. *How can I possibly eliminate any of these options?* It was an impossible task, and yet one she was expected to make as if it were a routine decision she made on a daily basis. It just wasn't her style to be doing any of this.

Finally, already feeling like she was about to burst from eating so much, Lauren appeared. Stephanie watched as Lauren took in the scene before her, eyes widening as she surveyed all the women, the cakes, the food, the fabric swatches, all of it. Stephanie could see the look of understanding spread over Lauren's face. *Now she understands why I need to be rescued from all this.*

Lauren immediately went over to Grann and gave her a big hug and kiss on the cheek. "Hi Grann! How are you?" Grann just gave her a smile and wink.

Stephanie's mom greeted Lauren. "Hello dear. We are *busy*, but very happy. Are you here to assist with the wedding planning? We need all the help we can get!"

"No, mom," Stephanie quickly said, "She's here to take me to lunch. We're going to catch up and then I'll be back."

Frowning at this news, Stephanie's mother said, "But wait, we have all this food here, and much more work to do today."

Stephanie grabbed Lauren by the arm and began to back pedal toward the doorway, saying, "We won't be long, okay?"

"But Stephy—" her mom began.

From the doorway, Stephanie addressed all the women in the room. "Thank you all so much. The dishes were all delicious and I wish we could have every single cake. I appreciate all your help and I can't wait to see you again at the wedding." Backing out the doorway, Stephanie and Lauren turn and make a run for it.

Hand-in-hand they ran out the front door where Lauren's Jeep, no doors or windows, awaited them. They jumped in, Lauren started the engine, cranked up the music, and said, "You ready, girl?"

Stephanie squealed in delight and said, "Just like old times, sis!"

Lauren punched the gas pedal and off they went.

CHAPTER 8

At the Château 1804's restaurant, Mr. Durant, Patrick, and Michael are at a table in the outdoor seating area, surrounded by meticulously well-kept gardens. Well-trained waiters buzz around the tables, bringing plates of chef-prepared food to patrons.

Patrick was all ears as Mr. Durant explained more about this establishment. "So, this establishment is the fourth hotel I bought and remodeled back in 2012 after the big earthquake. It's actually my favorite property, and the food here is incredible—French cuisine of course.

And we've had some great articles written about us in a few food magazines."

Thoroughly impressed by everything he had seen so far, Patrick said, "It's incredible. Exactly how many restaurants do you own?"

Mr. Durant thought for a moment before replying, "Right now, we have six restaurants but will have a seventh next summer."

"Wow, seven restaurants," Patrick said. "Plus this hotel.

"That's not all son," Mr. Durant went on, "I have ownership in a lot of companies. There's Papo food company, a telecommunications company, PAP security, and I have an ownership interest in Island TV as well."

Shaking his head in disbelief, Patrick said, "That is very impressive, sir. Stephanie never even mentioned any of this."

With a wave of his hand, Mr. Durant said, "After the wedding, I'll take you to the headquarters of each company." When he noticed Michael texting on his cell phone, he was clearly annoyed and scolded him. "Can you please put your cell phone away? It's quite rude to be on your phone at a dinner table."

Michael put his phone away, saying, "I just had to respond to a quick text."

Mr. Durant sighed with disapproval and turned his attention back to his lunch.

Patrick asked him, "How did you get into the food business?"

"Well, my father owned a small house he eventually turned into a bed and breakfast. When I was a kid, people who came to travel throughout the country would come and stay with us. My mother's cooking, which you experienced last night, became very popular as everyone loved her food, so people would come and stay just to eat my mother's cooking. After some years, word got around about my father's house and my mother's food, so more and more people came. My father had to get a bigger place every other year because we kept expanding and expanding. After about eight years of success, an English businessman came around who had heard about the food and stayed with us for a whole month. He loved the place, and of course the food, so he made my father an offer. He would invest in a bigger establishment, more of a hotel, and partner with my father if he ran the business. A few years after that, the Englishman passed away in a diving accident, leaving the entire business to my father."

"That's wonderful," Patrick said even as he realized that didn't sound right. "I mean, tragic for him, but amazing for your family.

"Yes, exactly," Mr. Durant continued, "My father put me and my brothers, who you'll meet soon, to work, and we all grew up working in the restaurant and the hotel business. After the success of that hotel, I decided to invest in a smaller hotel, a boutique hotel. That one became successful, so I got another one and another one, and here we are today."

He pulled out one of his cigars and lit it before continuing, "Our hotels are owned by us Haitians, not by other corporations. And we're very proud of them."

"That's inspiring," Patrick said. "And to think it all started with your mother's good food."

* * * * *

Over the course of the afternoon, Stephanie and Lauren visited all their old hangout spots, catching up on lost time. They wandered the streets, went to the marketplace, visited multiple bars, and popped into many shops and boutiques along the way. Stephanie was the happiest she'd felt yet since coming back to Haiti. Now they sat on a pristine white-sand beach, staring out at the ocean. No one else was around as this was a private beach, and it was one of their favorite secret spots. Laruen pulled two beers out of her purse and handed one to Stephanie.

"Yes!" Stephanie exclaimed. "You read my mind. I was just thinking we needed a drink."

"Girl, you *definitely* need one," Lauren said, which made them both burst into laughter.

Twisting off the caps, they clinked their bottles together and each took a sip. Lauren sighed and said, "I really miss you. I miss this."

Stephanie nodded her head, feeling the same way. "Me too. When did life get so complicated? I miss things being simple like this."

Lauren frowned and said, "It's called adulting, and if I would have known things would be like this, I wouldn't have been in such a rush to grow up."

"Tell me about it," Stephanie agreed. After staring a while longer at the ocean, she went on, "You need to come to Miami. I've been inviting you for months, you know."

With a guilty look on her face, Lauren said, "I know but I've been so busy, and to be honest, money has been pretty tight."

Turning to look her best friend in the face, Stephanie said, "Why didn't you say anything? Do you need some money? You know I'm happy to help, right?"

Lauren shook her head and said, "No, I'm fine. I am getting by here just fine, but traveling isn't in my budget right now."

"What if I buy you a plane ticket?" Stephanie asked. "Would you come then?"

Lauren wrapped her arm around Stephanie's shoulder and smiled. "Now *that* I can accept. Maybe I'll come to this other wedding ceremony you're talking about."

Stephanie put her head in her hands and moaned. "Oh my God, please don't remind me. I don't want to talk about any weddings today. I just want to breathe and be present here."

"Come on, I can't believe you don't want to talk about it at all," Lauren said with a look of concern on her face. "Is it really that stressful?"

Raising her head, Stephanie said, "Yes, girl. It's too much. I mean, I knew I had to get back here to visit, but I was more excited just to come home. I've missed everything so much."

Lauren was clearly a bit mystified by this. "Then why don't you come more often?

Stephanie sighed and thought for a moment before responding, "Because I've been so involved with Patrick." Shaking her head she continued, "That's no excuse, I know. I need to come home more, especially to see Grann."

"Yes," Lauren said, grabbing Stephanie's hand and squeezing it tight, "and especially if this place makes you happy. You were dying to get here so bad you had to use a wedding as an excuse to get home. That says something, you know."

"I was *not* using the wedding as an excuse to come," Stephanie said indignantly, but then smiled and added, "But it was the perfect reason to come back."

"I get it," Lauren agreed. "What is it about the wedding that's stressing you out so much? If I can help, just let me know."

Stephanie had been trying to answer this same question herself from the moment she arrived home. "I don't know, I can't explain it. It's probably just my overbearing mother, which is so ridiculous because she has never cared about *anything* I did, yet the moment I say I'm getting married, she's been non-stop." As if on cue, her phone rings for what feels like the thousandth time that afternoon. "She won't stop calling me and it's just way too much."

Nodding her head in agreement, Lauren said, "Sure, your mom has been a handful since we were kids, so that's nothing new. I really don't like to see you all stressed out like this."

Stephanie leaned over and hugged her friend tightly. "It's just, I don't know, I just feel so *weird* about everything."

Lauren looked into her eyes and said, "I mean, are you *happy*?

After a thoughtful pause, Stephanie replied, "Yeah, I guess. We have a really good time together."

"But you've only known him for such a short amount of time," Lauren prodded. "Are you worried about that at all?"

"Maybe I should be," Stephanie said, "but no, I'm not."

"Okay, I just had to ask," Lauren said. After a beat she added, "Because honestly, seeing you made my heart so full, but your energy was so low. You just don't seem like the old Stephanie. It's like something has changed. And it's okay, you know, to change and grow, but you just seem unhappy to me."

Since Lauren was her best friend and was genuinely interested in her wellbeing, Stephanie decided to come clean and lay all her cards on the table. "I feel like I'm always living someone else's version of my life. I'm just gonna let the sun hit me and exhale for a little bit." She leaned back on the sand and closed her eyes.

* * * * *

Patrick simply can't understand Michael's lackadaisical attitude about his father's businesses. He looked over at him and said, "Hey man, why aren't you interested in all of this?"

Michael opened his mouth to speak but instead his father interrupted him and said, "Michael has spent all his time trying to be a pop star. Music is all he cares about. That and hopping around the island, having a good time. That's all he's interested in."

Michael shook his head, ignoring his father again to provide his own answer to Patrick. "Actually brother, I never wanted to be a pop star. I am a musician. My band and I have been together for seven years. We go all over the country playing for the people. But I also do a lot of charity work. I work with homeless children and work to rebuild our country because there's still a lot of devastation here in Haiti since the last earthquake. I work to feed and clothe people. I make sure the hungry people can eat. That's how I spend my time."

Mr. Durant clearly wasn't interested in Michael's speech at all as he was more focused on re-lighting his cigar. Patrick, on the other hand, was genuinely interested in what Michael had to say. "Nice! I can't wait to hear your music. And the charity work is very admirable."

"That could be admirable," Mr. Durant said, "but not if you can't take care of yourself. You can't take care of everyone else and not have enough money to buy yourself a home. You know what they say on the airplane, put on *your* face mask first, and *then* help others with their mask. Well, Michael has a great big heart, but I wish his brain was as big as his heart. If it were, he could be very wealthy and have other people do his charity for him."

Michael sighed in exasperation and said, "I don't want anyone to do my charity for me. I like being with the people, and I like getting my hands dirty. You should try it and see how it feels because it actually feels very good when you help people directly instead of just paying others to do it for you, if you do it at all." Patrick was beginning to feel uncomfortable with Michael's direct attack on his father.

With a steely expression, Mr. Durant returned fire. "Oh, I know exactly how it feels. You know why? Because *you* are my charity. That truck you're driving, your home, and almost everything you own, I gave to you. So, I know exactly what it feels like to give without receiving anything in return."

Hoping Michael would back down a little, Patrick was disappointed to see he was clearly just getting revved up into being fully annoyed by his father. "Okay, father, you win. Yes, you got me the truck. But if I remember correctly, it was a birthday gift, because you were trying to bribe me into running this hotel. The thing is, when you give a gift it should come from your heart, not as a strategy to get someone to do what you want them to do. But that seems to be your specialty, so I see why you tried it. Just doesn't work on me."

"Of course not. Nothing works on you," Mr. Durant said with a sneer. "The word *work* and you shouldn't even be in the same sentence. You don't know anything about work and sadly, that's gonna bite you in the end."

Michael leaned forward and spoke with a level intensity Patrick hadn't seen in him before. He was seething mad but kept his voice low so others around them couldn't hear. "Maybe it will, maybe it won't. What I do know is when it's my time to meet the good Lord, I can look back on my life and be very pleased and happy with all the people I helped."

Patrick was horrified to be caught in the middle of this conflict. Not one to be intimidated by anyone, Mr. Durant leaned right in close to Michael's face, also keeping his voice at a discreet level. "Yes, me too. I can look back on my life and think of all the people I employ with these hotels, the family I provided for, and the children I have. I provide for you and your sister and neither of you have interest in this business. And that's fine, but neither one of you have what it takes to build your own business either. If you had your own successful business I could at least respect that. But you have nothing going on. At least your sister has flown out of the nest and is getting married and settling down to have a family. You, on the other hand, you just run around with all the women in the island. You've got poor Joseline chasing after you because she thinks you're a grown up but you're still just a boy. When you do finally grow up, you'll see how I'm right about this."

Having reached his limit, Michael jumped up from the table, knocking over his chair. He turned to very specifically only address Patrick. "Hey man, I'm not for all this bullshit. Text me when you're ready to see the *real* Haiti." With that, he stormed out of the restaurant.

Patrick didn't know what to say, so he sat in silence. Inexplicably, Mr. Durant had a devilish grin on his face, as if he got some kind of perverse pleasure from the argument. In a flash, Michael reappeared and slapped a $100 bill on the table and said, "Just because I no longer want your charity. I can pay for my own damn meal," then stormed off again.

Patrick could see other patrons had been watching all this take place and was thoroughly embarrassed on behalf of the family. Mr. Durant laughed loudly, shrugged his shoulders, and said, "This isn't the first time he's behaved like this. He'll be upset, he'll cool off, and then he'll call me when he needs more money." Mr. Durant acted as if nothing even happened and casually changed the subject. "So, let's talk about your tech expertise. I might need someone like you for my businesses."

Relieved to focus anything other than what just happened, Patrick was especially happy to have a chance to speak about his own skills. "Great! Ask me anything you want to know."

CHAPTER 9

As Lauren pulled the Jeep into the driveway of the Durant residence, Stephanie was feeling more relaxed and carefree than she had felt in a long time. Reclining in the passenger seat, she noticed they had pulled up behind Michael's Land Cruiser. Then she saw Michael and her mother standing near the front door. They were having what appeared to be a very tense interaction. When Lauren turned the Jeep off, they could both hear them.

Michael threw his hands up in disgust and said, "I don't want anything he's ever given me. I'm *done*! So, Mom, here are the keys to the truck." He held them out to her, but she wouldn't take them.

Stephanie's mother was trying to calm him down. "Please come inside, Michael. Let's sit down as a family and talk about this."

"You think I can talk to that man?" Michael practically yelled. "He's ridiculous. He thinks the charity work I do makes me a weak man. I don't want anything to do with him anymore."

Casually, Stephanie's dad opened the front door and leaned against the jamb, watching the argument, as did Stephanie from a safe distance in Lauren's Jeep.

"I hear you," Michael's mother was saying, now in tears. "But this truck was a gift from *me*, not him. It was *my* gift to you, so please take it."

Michael wasn't having any of it. "Yeah, right. Your gift that *he* paid for, Mom. He got me the gift. I don't want anything from him. And I don't want to be in the hotel business, okay? There are bigger fish to fry than that—*real* people with *real* problems who need help. This country has been falling apart for years, and while he's sitting on the sidelines making millions of dollars, the rest of the country is starving!" He turned and addressed his father directly. "Do you even *know* that?"

Stepping from the door toward Michael, his father said, "Do I know what? That the country would be starving even more if I didn't hire all these people to work for me? Who do you think cleans the hotel rooms? Who hires the janitors and maids that clean the hotel rooms? Who hires the cooks in the kitchen? These people can eat, and their families can eat because of people like me. So don't you dare think I don't contribute to this country. I contribute more than you could ever dream of."

Stephanie watched her mother stepped in front of her husband so he didn't get any closer to his son.

"That's right, throw money at them," Michael fired back. "Give them jobs that pay them below minimum wage and now they're free? Even with those jobs these people are suffering. You know nothing of these people, the ones who go to work sick and in pain and work so hard for you. It takes them all year to make what you make in a week, and you think you're doing them such a big favor? This is the problem I have with you. You're just like the French were. All you care about is money, not even family. When was last time you took mom out to dinner? Or did something nice for her? Everything is about money with you. And that's fine if that's how you want to live your life. But I won't *ever* live my life like that."

Because his mother wouldn't accept the keys to his Land Cruiser, he threw them on the grass in front of them. "So, take your truck and I'll be bringing every gift you ever gave me back 'cuz I don't want anything to do with you. I'm done with *all* of it." He then turned and stomped away to Joseline's car, which was also parked in the driveway. Joseline was in the car, waiting for him.

With a final plea, his mother cries out, "Please, Michael!" But he just got into Joseline's car and they drove away. Stephanie watched as her mother sobbed and ran into the house, her father following close behind her. Slowly, Stephanie got out of the Jeep. There was always a lot of tension in the Durant household, but she hadn't seen this kind of blowup in years.

Lauren leaned over and said, "Call me if you need me, okay?"

Looking a bit dazed, Stephanie nodded her head and watched Lauren drive away. One slow step at a time she walked toward the front door, not looking forward to what else was in store inside. Where was Patrick in all this?

Once inside, she avoided her parents and went in search of Patrick. She found him in his bedroom, seated by the window, reading the Robb Report and sipping a glass of rum. He suddenly looked a lot like her father, and she wasn't at all sure how she felt about that in this moment. "Hey, what the hell happened today?"

Patrick took another sip of his rum and calmly responded, "Your brother is what happened. Your father was just talking to him about business, and I guess he got all pissed off over it. He stormed off and left the restaurant. Then when we came here, he brought his truck back. I guess your dad bought it for him? I don't know. He seems really crazy right now."

Stephanie felt her indignation rising. "What do you mean crazy? My brother's not crazy."

"I know he's not," Patrick said, "but your dad does have a point."

"What do you mean? What point? I don't even know what's going on."

Patrick thought for a moment and said, "Basically, your father's tired of your brother being lazy and living off him. And to be honest, I can't say that I blame him."

Now Stephanie could feel her face heating up in anger, but she tried to tamp it down. "Excuse me, lazy? Michael doesn't have a lazy bone in his body. Just because he doesn't do what my father wants him to do does *not* mean he's lazy!"

"Yeah but, think about it," Patrick continued, "He's a grown man living off your parents' money and he doesn't even want to help out at all with your father's business. That feels a little ungrateful to me."

That was the last straw for Stephanie. She knew exactly what Michael was going through because she herself had big tensions with her mother. Now she was mad as hell. "You know what? You don't even know what you're talking about, like at all! First, my brother has a heart of gold. He does so much for struggling people in this country. You literally have no idea what you're talking about. And while you've been here running around with my father kissing his ass, you should have taken time to really get to *know* my brother. But because he's not Mr. Moneybags, you apparently have no interest!"

Patrick was shocked at this outburst. "Kissing your father's ass? That's ridiculous! That's not accurate at all. I'm just being respectful of your father. Isn't that what you would expect me to do?"

"Yes," Stephanie agreed, but then turned the tables by saying, "but you know if you came to Haiti and my father was a goat herder and had no money and we lived in a shack, you would not be giving him the same energy you're giving him now."

Patrick's hesitation before answering was all the confirmation she needed. They both knew she was right. Still, Patrick tried to deny it. "Please. I would treat him exactly the same way."

Stephanie wasn't having it. "You're so impressed with my father, this house, and his wealth, but you can't even see *me* right now! Can you not see how completely stressed out I am?"

With a genuine look of concern on his face, Patrick said, "What do you mean? You're not happy?"

Stephanie heaved a sigh and paced back and forth. "I don't know. I don't feel right. All this pressure my parents are putting on me. I managed to forget it's why I even left Haiti to begin with, which was to get away from them! And I *really* don't like how you're reminding me a *lot* of my father right now. I definitely *do not* want that. I don't want someone who just cares about appearances. I want *substance*."

Now it was Patrick's turn to feel indignant. "So, you don't think our relationship has substance?"

"I'm just saying you don't ever ask me anything about what *I'm* doing in my life," Stephanie tried to explain. "Like my jewelry business. Do you know the latest piece I just launched? Do you even know what's happening in two months back in Miami?"

With probably more attitude than he intended, Patrick replied, "I don't know, but I have a feeling you're going to tell me."

She could have punched him in the face at that moment. Instead, she took a breath and said, "Saks Fifth Avenue is going to be looking at my jewelry. I've been working my ass off to get it all together so after this wedding I can pitch to them and hopefully be accepted and have my jewelry available in their stores."

Patrick smiled despite the tension and said, "That's great! But I can't believe you didn't *tell* me."

"My point," Stephanie continued, "is I can't believe *you* never bothered to ask what was happening in *my* life. All we ever talk about is *your* life, *your* business, *your* success. I had to basically twist your arm to even get you to come to Haiti. And I know if you knew about my father's wealth, you would have been itching to get down here a long time ago."

"That's not fair, Stephanie, and you know it," Patrick argued back. "You don't know how I would be if you were poor. And remember, I asked you to marry me when I didn't know about any of this, so stop it with this money bullshit."

Stephanie wasn't about to give up or give in now. "All I'm saying is before you sit here and judge my brother and think you know everything about him, why don't you take time to get to know him? You don't know everything about my father, either. You don't know the ways he put our family on the back burner, or the way he treated my mother, all in the name of success. So, think about that before you start judging people you barely know."

Patrick also wasn't interested in just folding and said, "What I know is that he's been able to provide for you and your family in a way most people only dream of."

Raising her voice a couple more notches, Stephanie said, "That's right. This big house, the cars, the hotels, the money. He has provided all of it but guess what, no one's here! This big house is empty!" She was now fighting hard to hold back the tears she knew would come if she pursued this direction in which she was headed. *Time to take a break*. "You know what? I need to go see if my brother's okay. I gotta get out of here."

As she slipped out the bedroom door, she heard Patrick call after her, "Wait!" but kept going. She needed to clear her head, and she did want to check in on her brother.

CHAPTER 10

Stephanie made her way to a bar where she was sure she'd find Michael. Inside was a festive atmosphere with music playing and people drinking and dancing. She spied a couple men playing dominoes and when they saw her, they whistled at her. Stephanie realized one of them is Joseline's father, Dwight Chapoteau, an average man in his fifties with silver hair and beard. As he squinted in her direction, a look of recognition came to his face.

"Aren't you the Durant girl?" he asked. "Where you been these last few years?"

"Hello, Mr. Chapoteau," she said warmly.

Looking her up and down, admiring her beauty, he said, "Hello to you! How old are you now?"

Stephanie rolled her eyes and got right to the point. "Have you seen Michael?"

Still grinning and eyeing her, he responded, "Umm hmm."

Enough of this you dirty old man. "Well? Where?"

Mr. Chapoteau pointed to another section of the bar and said, "They're over there."

The kind of men who frequented this bar weren't used to seeing women like Stephanie in there and they weren't shy about staring at her. Ignoring them, she walked deeper into the bar to find her brother. He was on the stage, of course, performing his heart out, singing and playing his guitar. She sees Joseline sitting to one side, watching him in awe, as if he was singing only for her. As she watched, Stephanie realized she'd forgotten just how talented a musician her brother was.

When the song ended, Michael put his guitar away and came down off the stage. Stephanie was surprised to see none other than Hip Hop star Troubleboy Hitmaker shaking Michael's hand and congratulating him for such a great performance. *I can't believe Troubleboy is here and talking to my brother. That's fantastic!* She watched as Michael then took Joseline by the hand and led her to the bar to get drinks. Stephanie walked up behind him and tapped him on the shoulder. He turned and looked surprised to see her, asking, "What are you doing here? How did you find me?"

Stephanie replied, "First of all that was so dope! And Troubleboy Hitmaker giving you some love? Wow!"

"Thank you," he said with a smile.

"I know your spots, you know," Stephanie went on, "Granted, I had to go to the other three first but hey, I found you." Turning to Joseline she said, "Hey Joseline. Nice to see you." To her brother she said, "I'm sorry about what happened."

Michael frowned and said, "Yeah, me too," but then changed his mind and said, "Actually no, I'm not sorry this time. This was bound to happen sooner or later, so I'm glad."

"Yes, but why did it have to happen like this? Stephanie asked with sadness in her eyes and voice."

Trying to shake it off, Michael said, "It's all good. I'm not even worried about it, you know? Dad has been who he is for years, and I've put up with it for so long, but no more. I'm done. I don't want anything to do with him."

"Yeah, but he *is* our father. You can't just cut him off like that."

"Why can't I? You think he thinks about anyone other than himself?"

"Well, I can't disagree with you on that point."

"Of course not. The thing is, he has this idea that somehow I'm a loser. And it's crazy, but when I'm around him, I view myself that way too. But when I'm out in the streets with my people I feel alive. That's when I feel more like myself than anywhere else, and also when I'm with her," Michael said, gesturing to Joseline. Stephanie can tell he's been drinking enough that he's a bit tipsy and speaking very openly. "She's my best friend. She *knows* who I am."

Stephanie was worried for her brother. "Dad has been letting you live at the one of the hotels, right? So, what are you gonna do now?"

Still gazing lovingly at Joseline he replied, "I'm moving in with her. She said I could stay with her until I get on my feet."

"That's very sweet of you," Stephanie said to Joseline. *Well, at least she obviously is head over heels for him. I can at least be happy about that.*

Michael turned to Stephanie and said, "And don't worry. Dad's not gonna stop me from coming to your wedding, okay? You don't have to worry about that."

"That's not why I came here," Stephanie explained to him. "I just wanted to make sure you're okay."

"I'm good," Michael said, as if trying to convince himself. "Trust me. This is a good thing."

"Good," Stephanie said, then added, "Besides, I don't even want to *think* about the wedding right now."

Now she had Michael's full attention. He regarded her for a moment, then said, "Can I ask you something? Why are you marrying Patrick?"

This caught Stephanie slightly off-guard. "What do you mean, *why*?"

Michael chose his words carefully, saying, "I mean, what do you see in him?"

"You don't like him?" Stephanie asked.

"No, that's not it," Michael replied. "He's a nice enough guy and all, but you two just don't quite seem to fit right."

Stephanie couldn't fathom what he was getting at. "What do you mean by that?"

Michael shrugged and said, "I just mean he is a lot like dad. And I never thought you would be with someone like that. I'm surprised you don't see it."

Now it was Stephanie's turn to think for a moment, considering what Michael just shared. "I mean, I know he's a businessman, but he has a very playful side too, and he has a sweet side, and we have fun together."

"Yeah, that's all fine and dandy," Michael explained, "but fun runs out, you know. Does he know who you are? Does he know what you love? You love this country like nothing else. Does he know you're an island girl who would rather have flip flops on than heels? I just see you as a different person with him. Even the way you dress, it's all different.

Somewhere deep inside Stephanie knows Michael is right and finds the thought depressing. *Shit. I need a drink.* She gestured to the bartender, an old man who looked like he'd been working there forever. He hobbled over to their end of the bar and Stephanie said, "Excuse me, can I have whatever he's having?" The bartender poured her some rum and slid it over to her. She grabbed the drink and downed it. She saw the look of surprise on Michael's face and said, "Look, I'm stressed out, okay?"

Michael went on to say, "Listen, sis. I'm down for you, and whatever you want to do in your life, but marriage is a huge commitment. You guys haven't even known each very long. Before you make the same mistake as mom did, be sure you know his heart really well. More importantly, make sure he knows yours."

Joseline finally spoke up and said, "On that note, bartender! Three shots of Toast!"

The three of them laugh together and the tension eases. *Wedding planning be damned.* Stephanie was all in and just wanted to drink, dance, and enjoy the company of her brother and his girlfriend.

* * * * *

Stephanie feels a hand lightly tapping her check and playfully tugging on her ear. Not even half awake, she mumbled, "Go away. I'm sleeping."

Michael's voice cut through her grogginess as he said, "Sis, you gotta wake up."

It took a huge effort on her part, but Stephanie managed to pull herself up into a sitting position and open her eyes. She was on a small couch in a rather tiny apartment. It was very "girly" and modern. Pictures of Michael and Joseline were all over the place. Clearly, this was Joseline's place, though

Stephanie couldn't remember ever being there before. Then again, she couldn't remember how she got here either. She put her throbbing head in her hands and moaned. She hadn't been hung over like this in a very long time. *Why do people even drink in the first place? This is awful.* Then reality hit her and she said, "Oh my god, what time is it?"

"It's time for you to call mom and Patrick," Michael replied. "Everybody's going crazy looking for you."

"How did I end up here?" she asked, trying to remember.

Michael filled in the necessary details. "You got drunk at the bar, and I couldn't let you drive home. Shit, I almost couldn't even drive myself. So, of course, I brought you back here. Your phone has been going off all morning. Twenty-six messages from mom. The last couple were from Patrick."

Joseline brought her a big glass of water with two Tylenol and said, "Here, take this."

"Thank you. You really are the sweetest. And the best sister I never had," Stephanie said, truly grateful for her presence.

This made Joseline smile and say, "No worries. Let me know if you want some food."

The thought of food made Stephanie queasy. "No, I better get home before they send out a search party for me."

"Yes," Michael agreed, "and I'm going to drive you home because I don't think you're in a good place to drive."

Stephanie agreed and said, "No, I'm not. My head is still spinning."

"Exactly. Come on, let's go," Michael said, then grinned and added, "I'll stop and grab some greasy food for you."

Downing the rest of her water, Stephanie shot him a look that said *don't even think about it.*

* * * * *

As Michael drove toward home in Joseline's car with Stephanie, they were both quiet and deep in thought. Finally, Stephanie turned to Michael and said, "But you love your truck."

Michael nodded in agreement and said, "Yeah, and?"

"Why give it back to dad? You know it's only going to sit there in the driveway."

"It's deeper than that," Michael explained.

"Yes, I know," Stephanie went on, "but it's how you get around to do all your charity work. Screw dad. Take the truck and still give him the finger. God knows you've earned it dealing with all his nonsense over the years."

"Shit, in that case I've earned ten trucks!" Michael joked. They both had a good laugh over that one.

Stephanie needed to get serious with him. There was a point she wanted to make. "Can I ask you something now?"

Michael looked nervous. "Maybe? Depends on the question." Stephanie rolled her eyes and he added, "Seriously. Okay, shoot."

"Why haven't you ever committed to Joseline?"

Looking surprised by the question, Michael said, "What are you talking about?"

Stephanie continued, "You guys have been on-and-off since high school, but she's perfect for you."

Michael gave a scoffing kind of look and said, "Please, she's my best friend."

"Exactly!" Stephanie exclaimed.

"It's good just the way it is," Michael said, looking unsure where this line of inquiry was headed.

"I look around her apartment, and I see pictures of you and her everywhere. I mean, clearly this woman is so in love with you. And I think she just hangs around because she'd rather have *some* piece of you than *no* piece of you, which makes me sad because she *should* have *all* of you. You guys are really great together."

Michael shrugged and said, "I don't think marriage is for me, so you get married first and then give me some advice."

Stephanie laughed and said, "That's fair. Listen, I know you have your feelings about marriage because of mom and dad but we don't have to have marriages like theirs."

"Ugh," Michael frowned and said, "I'd rather die than have a marriage like that."

"I know, right?" Stephanie agreed. "But for real. This woman volunteers with you. She's smart and has a freaking PhD. I mean, come on! And she's so beautiful. I know mom and dad don't really approve because her family's poor, but who cares? She is the woman for you, and you would be crazy *not* to marry her. Don't think she's going to be around forever because she won't be. I mean, she just had a date with someone else, right?"

Michael reflected on that for a moment before answering. "Yeah, I know. And I'm not taking advantage, but she is my best friend and right now that works for us."

"Okay," Stephanie said with a sigh.

He reached over and gave her a playful little shove on the shoulder and said, "And you got your nerve talking to me about marriage! You should ask yourself all the things you just asked me. And *then* you and I can have a talk about Joseline."

Stephanie looked out the window and mumbled, "Whatever." *He's right, of course.*

CHAPTER 11

As Michael pulled into the driveway of the Durant resident, their parents and Patrick all rushed out the front door. Stephanie was mortified and knew this was going to be a huge scene. She dreaded it, but it was also necessary. Slowly, she and Michael got out of the car. *Time to face the music, I guess.*

Her mom rushed forward first, clearly livid. "Stephanie, how could you leave and not tell any of us where you were and be gone all night?"

Instead of his usual silence, her father chimed in, "I'm very disappointed in you Stephanie. You could have at least called. We were worried sick."

Stephanie looked at Patrick, who didn't say anything at all, but the look on his face spoke volumes. *He agrees with them. I should have known he would.* She walked straight past all of them and headed for the house. At the door, she paused to look back at her brother.

Michael turned to get back in Joseline's car and leave, but his mother had a look on her face that said she meant business as she said, "Don't you even *think* about leaving here." With a resigned sigh, he followed Stephanie as she went into the house.

Stephanie went straight to the kitchen and got a jar of guava juice from the fridge. She gulped down the entire jar as her parents, Michael, and Patrick came in behind her.

Her mom picked up where they had left off outside, saying, "Seriously. Where have you been all night?"

With an indignant tone she said, "Mom, I went to check on Michael since no one else was going to do it. I had a few drinks and obviously drank too much. He took me back to Joseline's to rest. And now I'm here. Okay?"

Her father added, "You've clearly been gone a long time because you seem to have forgotten you don't talk to me or your mother this way!"

Stephanie moans and squeezes her temples in frustration. Her head is still throbbing.

"We're going above and beyond to give you the perfect wedding and do everything for you," her mother said. "We don't deserve to be treated like this."

"I didn't ask you to go above and beyond," Stephanie said. "This is *your* dream. This is what *you've* been waiting for my whole life, and you've never cared this much about anything else in my life. You want me to get married, have children, and be the perfect little wife, just like you. But that's not for me!"

Stephanie can see her mother is both shocked and offended by her words. "I just want you to be happy. That's all!"

Closing her eyes and taking a deep breath, Stephanie said, "What makes me happy is designing jewelry. But you never even ask me about that. You guys don't care about *anything* Michael and I do unless it's in line with *your* desires for us. Do you even know the extent of all the charity work Michael does for the people in this country?"

"Your brother is not the topic of this conversation right now, you are," her father said firmly.

"Yes, I know," Stephanie said, trying to maintain her composure. "Look, I'm sorry you were worried, but I needed this. I needed to talk to Michael and to get away and think about some things."

Her mother then said, "Well, I hope your mind is clear now and that you're ready to get back to work, because we have more people coming to go over the designs for the table. Plus, we've got to go over the seating chart."

Waving her off, Stephanie said, "Yeah, fine, mom. I just can't talk about this right now. I need to lay down and rest."

After her mother stormed out of the kitchen, Grann slowly walked in, looking around with a confused look on her face. "What is all the fuss about?"

"I didn't come home last night because I stayed with Michael," Stephanie explained, "but I didn't call and worried everyone. That was wrong and I'm sorry."

Looking for a target for his own anger, her father turned to Michael and said, "How could you let this happen? You're her brother! You should be looking out for your sister and making sure she's okay."

Stephanie could see Michael was trying to contain his anger to avoid a repeat of yesterday's explosive encounter.

"And that's exactly what I did, Dad," Michael said in a strained tone. "I made sure she was safe. I took her home and made sure she slept well. Then I got her back here safely. Is that man enough for you?"

Her father shot right back with, "Don't take that tone with me in my house."

Stephanie couldn't take it anymore and directed her frustration at her father. "Stop! Please, Dad. Stop treating him like that. Aren't you tired of this? Instead of always trying to force him to do what you want him to do and follow your path, why don't you even try to see what he's interested in for a change?" Her father was surprised by this and fell silent, so she added, "Why don't you take a day off work and go with him around the island to his charities? Why don't you step into *his* shoes for once? You keep trying to get him to step into your shoes, can't you try stepping into his, just once?"

Her father folded his arms in a classic gesture of defiance and said, "I don't need to put myself in his shoes. I have—"

"No, Daddy," Stephanie said, cutting him off, "You need to find common ground with your *son*. The one thing you guys have in common is how you both love your family. That's why he took care of me last night. And that's why you're doing all of this for me. So instead of always talking about your differences, why don't you talk about what you have in common? Maybe you can have a relationship with your son, and not lose him."

Stephanie could see Michael loves how she is giving it to their father. Even Grann was nodding her head in agreement, which gave her more confidence. But she also knew her father was incredibly stubborn. Now he pulled out the "sacrificial parent" card and played it hard. "Listen, I have done everything for both of you kids. *Everything*! I worked hard for years to make sure you didn't want for anything. That's the sacrifice I've made for this family."

"And we appreciate all that you've done," Stephanie said with sincerity. "You know that. But with everything you've done, we only ask for the simplest thing—Just *listen* to us. Hear about what we have in *our* hearts and what *our* desires are. If you showed just the tiniest bit of interest, it would change *everything*." Her father is once again silent. *Is he softening up to the idea?* "You guys need to take some time to talk. Lovingly. Right now, Patrick and I need to talk. Please excuse us." She gestures for Patrick to follow her to the deck. He is quiet and doesn't say a word as he follows her.

They stood by the table her father sat at when Patrick first met him. He is clearly still upset by her disappearing act. *Time for some damage control.* "Look, I'm really sorry you were worried about me last night."

"Well, you should be," he said indignantly. "I haven't slept at all."

"I know, and I really am sorry," Stephanie said. "I meant to text you to say we were going to have a couple of drinks. And you know I don't drink, so it hit me hard and I got wasted. I'm so sorry."

Patrick added, "And we still need to talk about everything that happened yesterday."

"I know," Stephanie agreed. "We do need to figure some things out before we go through with this."

Slowly pacing around the deck, Patrick said, "I stayed up all night thinking about what you said to me yesterday, and you're right. I *am* impressed with your father and your family. But more than the success or the money or the luxury lifestyle, the most important thing is I love you."

Stephanie put a hand on his shoulder to look him in the eyes. "And I love you too, Patrick. But marriage isn't just about love. It's also about *compatibility.*"

"I know you're the right person for me," Patrick said. "And I want to make you happy. I know we can have an amazing, successful marriage."

"But how do you know that?" Stephanie asked. "How do you know it'll be successful?"

"I just know," Patrick replied, shaking his head. "I can't explain it."

Stephanie sighed and said, "I feel like you want me because I am exactly what you see your colleagues have, a trophy wife. I know you think I'm beautiful, but there's so much more to me than my appearance. Just like my father, you show no interest in my dreams and the things I'm passionate about. That's a big red flag for me."

She can see Patrick knows she's right, but he still stood his ground. "You're right. I have been so focused this last year on developing my work that I haven't taken time to learn what you love. And I'm sorry. But I do want to know and be involved in your dreams too."

"Good, because there is still so much more you need to learn about me," she explained. "Haiti is my home, and although you see all this wealth, there's another side of this country that isn't so polished, but it's still a big part of me. I'm deeply rooted in that as well. You need to know *all* sides of me, including the sides that aren't so beautiful. I'm not going to be like your colleagues' wives, shopping all day and wearing tiny dresses and too much makeup."

Patrick had to chuckle at that and said, "I never asked you to be that. I don't even want that."

Stephanie continued, "I'm just saying, I see the world you live in. You admire my father and the men you work with. Their wives are just like my mother, gorgeous arm candy. They stay at home and make sure the house is beautiful and everything looks good while you go live your dreams. I can't live like that."

Grabbing her hand and squeezing it tightly, Patrick said, "And I would never ask you to. I want your dreams to come true too."

Time to lay all my cards on the table. "My dream is directly tied to Haiti. I finally know what I want to do. I'm going to hire people in my own country to make my jewelry, which means I'll be back and forth between here and Miami quite often. Is that something you can live with?"

Patrick was surprisingly quick to respond, saying, "Of course. I support you."

Does this mean we're finally on the same page after all this time? She smiled and said, "Good, but there's just a lot more I think we should discover about each other *before* we do this. That's all I'm saying."

With a crestfallen look, Patrick said, "So, you don't want to get married?"

"No, of course I do," Stephanie replied, "but maybe we need to have some more time."

"I'm ready, Steph. I don't need any more time because I know what I want," Patrick said, but after only a slight pause he added, "But, I'll wait if that's what *you* want."

Stephanie was happy to finally hear this. She held his face in her hands and stared deeply into his eyes. She loved him more in this moment than ever before. "Thank you. I love you."

"I love you too," Patrick said. They kissed and held each in a long, loving embrace. Finally, Patrick pulled back slightly and said, "But your parents, they did all this planning for the wedding!"

Nodding her head in agreement, Stephanie said, "Yeah, I know. But I think that can be fixed." *In fact, I've got the perfect plan if I can pull it off.*

CHAPTER 12

The ballroom in Château 1804 was decked out with beautiful bright colors. Tropical flowers were everywhere. A band was on a stage playing Haitian music. Despite the vastness of the space, it was jam-packed with more than 200 tables, each with a gorgeous centerpiece made up of tropical flowers and greenery, along with perfectly appointed place settings.

Every table was fully occupied with formally dressed guests. One entire wall was lined with tables bearing every imaginable Haitian dish in a buffet like no one had ever seen. In the very center of the ballroom was an elegant round table with a massive, beautifully decorated wedding cake. The band began to play the traditional Haitian wedding song in preparation for the bride and groom to enter. Everyone stood and looked toward the ballroom doors in anticipation.

When the doors opened, it was Michael and Joseline who walked in. Joseline looked gorgeous in a traditional white gown of Haitian design. Michael was beaming with pride as they made their way to the center table and took their seats.

Stephanie and Patrick got up from their table and came over to greet the happy couple. Patrick gave Michael a big bear hug while Stephanie planted a loving kiss on Joseline's cheek. Returning to their table, Stephanie and Patrick both watched as Mr. Durant made his way over to Michael and Joseline. Michael rose to greet his father, who extended his hand to shake, but Michael, in typical fashion, gave him a big hug instead. Stephanie is truly moved as she watched her father fighting hard to hold back tears. *At last. A new chapter for those two.*

After many more people stop by the wedding table, Michael made his way to the stage, grabbed the microphone, and addressed the room. "Wow. All my people here. Thank you for coming to celebrate on such short notice. We love you guys. We couldn't do any of this without you. I would first like to thank my parents for all their support. But I especially want to thank my sister, who came home and helped restore our family. I would like to ask her to come and say a few words."

Startled, Stephanie froze, eyes wide. "Well, go on up there and say something," Patrick encouraged her.

Stephanie reluctantly walked up on the stage, took the microphone from Michael, inhaled deeply, and said, "Greetings, everyone. So, I'm not very good at this sort of thing, but I would just like to say that being away from your loved ones for a significant amount of time is difficult, but at the same time it gives you a chance to reflect on who you are as in individual. Life is complicated enough trying to satisfy one's own interests, let alone adding someone else to your equation. But every so often someone comes along and makes this difficult task worth the effort."

After pausing a moment to give a loving look to Patrick, she went on, "To my dear Joseline, the way I've watched you look at my brother over the years is how everyone should hope to be looked upon. I couldn't ask for a better sister I never had, so welcome to the family. To my beloved brother Michael, I've watched you grow from an overactive boy to a community-active man. Thank you for always staying true to yourself and making the best decision ever by marrying your best friend. To the bride and groom!"

Michael raised a glass of champagne and shouted, "To Haiti!"

The room erupted in cheers and whistles and the band kicked into high gear with upbeat Haitian music. Everyone was up and out of their seats dancing, even Grann. Despite the upbeat music, Stephanie and Patrick were in each other's arms slow dancing and gazing lovingly into one another's eyes.

~ THE END ~

ABOUT THE AUTHOR

Dieuveny "DJ" Jean Louis (aka "Mr. Toast") is a steadfast visionary in the spirits, restaurant, boating, music, and entertainment industries, and a Florida resident since the age of ten. Born in Haiti, DJ has built an array of highly successful businesses, all while becoming a philanthropic ambassador determined to change the world. DJ created Toast First Response, the corporate social responsibility division of Toast Distillers, Inc., a Miami-based spirits conglomerate he founded. It is best-known for its ultra-premium vodka, Toast™. It includes The Miami Distilling Company, where all its products are made. In 2016 Toast vodka was the official vodka of the 2017America's Cup and the 2017 Sundance Film Festival.

Toast Distillers specializes in developing brands internally, including Toast H2O alkaline purified water, as well as facilitating the branding and distribution needs of other specialty spirits and beverage companies. The company's products include a full range of ultra-premium to midline and well-line spirits products for vodka, rum, gin, tequila, whiskey, and Toast H2O. Products in development include wine and sparkling wine. For more information, email info@ toastdistillers.com, visit www.toastdistillers.com, or visit www.toastvodka.com.

DJ became increasingly well-connected with some of Miami's biggest stars, including Rick Ross and Pitbull. He pulled strings to leverage those celebrity relationships to help his community back in Haiti. On December 5, 2009, DJ threw his first major benefit concert, where Ross headlined a crowd of roughly 750,000. Just one month later on January 10, 2010, DJ had landed in Haiti at around noon, and then only a matter of hours later, a 7.0-magnitude earthquake hit, wreaking havoc and killing more than 200,000 people. He would have been one of those casualties if it weren't for his love of Haitian cuisine. Instead of settling into Hotel Montana, he dropped off his luggage and headed into town for some food. Everyone inside the hotel died during the quake. Narrowly escaping death is what inspired DJ to create Toast Vodka and its motto, "To life, to love, to us, because there is always a reason to Toast."

Passionate about the restaurant industry, DJ invested in the famous Miami Subs franchise. In 2011, as executive partner, he led the effort to rebrand the aging concept by recruiting Miami icons such as Pitbull to help fuel the expansion. His strategy doubled the number of owned and operated locations, with hundreds under license-contract worldwide.

DJ founded the record label Fast Life Entertainment in 2012 and Toast Vodka in 2014. He also founded *Re-Envision Magazine* in 2018, featuring an artistic fusion of art, music, fashion, and lifestyle through the eyes of an art enthusiast. Building on his love of the restaurant and entertainment industries, DJ established Kuba Cabana, a lively dining concept where old-world Cuba meets modern Miami. In 2017 DJ married luxury swimwear designer Anielka Mercado Jean Louis.

A Haitian Wedding is DJ's first novel as well as his first screenplay. The film premiered in December 2022 under the 1804 Studios label.

Follow DJ on Instagram: @MrToastworld

www.ingramcontent.com/pod-product-compliance
Lightning Source LLC
Chambersburg PA
CBHW030335310726
48979CB00001B/38

* 9 7 8 1 9 5 1 5 0 3 9 6 3 *